Once upon a time,

an evil circus owner named Bombax plotted to replace the king with a magical counterpart. You are Laela, a young person who first angers Bombax by freeing his pegasus, then earns his hatred by learning about his scheme. You must avoid the "accidents" Bombax arranges for you and at the same time decide which circus people you can trust.

What will you do?

You have been forced to perform a dangerous trapeze act with your friend Petra. As you feel yourself slipping from his grasp high above the center ring, you must make a choice:

1) You can let go and hope that you can somehow escape the death awaiting you. Turn to page 147.

2) You can hang on and hope for help. Turn to page 60.

3) Or you can grab the magic crystal tear hanging around your neck and summon a pegasus to your aid. Turn to page 16.

Whichever choice you make, you are sure to find adventure as you perform in the
CIRCUS OF FEAR

An ENDLESS QUEST™ Book   #10

CIRCUS of FEAR

BY ROSE ESTES

Cover Art by Keith Parkinson
Interior Art by Kevin Nichols

TSR Inc.

This book is for Tammi Hess
and every other girl
who would dare to be a heroine—
and for D.R. Miller
and the Carson & Barnes Circus

CIRCUS OF FEAR
©**copyright 1983 TSR Hobbies, Inc.**
All Rights Reserved.

Distributed to the book trade in the United States by Random
House, Inc. and in Canada by Random House of Canada, Ltd.
Distributed in the United Kingdom by TSR (UK), Ltd.
Distributed to the toy and hobby trade by regional distributors.

DUNGEONS & DRAGONS, ENDLESS QUEST, and PICK A
PATH TO ADVENTURE are trademarks owned by TSR
Hobbies, Inc.

D&D is a registered trademark owned by TSR Hobbies, Inc.

First Printing: July, 1983
Printed in the United States of America
Library of Congress Catalog Card Number: 83-50050
ISBN: 0-88038-037-3

9 8 7 6 5 4 3 2 1

TSR Hobbies, Inc.   TSR Hobbies (UK), Ltd.
P.O. Box 756   The Mill, Rathmore Road
Lake Geneva, WI 53147   Cambridge CB1 4AD
                        United Kingdom

ou are about to set off on a quest in which YOU will meet many dangers and face many decisions. YOUR choices will determine how the story turns out. So be careful . . . you must choose wisely!

Do not read this book from beginning to end! Instead, as you are faced with a decision, follow the instructions and keep turning to the pages where your choices lead you until you come to an end. At any point, YOUR choice could lead to success—or disaster!

You can read CIRCUS OF FEAR many times, with many different results, so if you make an unwise choice, go back to the beginning and start again.

Good luck on YOUR adventure!

In this story, you are Laela, a young person who is visiting the circus with Petra, a friend. You've come to see the performance in the big top, and the ringmaster is about to start the show. . . .

"Ladies and gentlemen and children of all ages! The Bombax Brothers' Circus of Fantasy is proud to present the largest collection of extraordinary performing monsters and mortals in the World of Greyhawk. They will astound, amaze, delight, and frighten you.

"And now we ask you to direct your attention to the mammoth steel arena in the center ring for a whirlwind of caged fury as black-maned caterwauls and ferocious displacer beasts—natural deadly enemies—perform under the direction of the incomparable Rebus Romney!"

"Hurry, Laela. It's starting. We're going to be late," Petra says angrily.

"I just can't leave. It's a sin to chain a pegasus. You go on, and I'll be there soon. I want to pet her a little longer."

"You! Children! What are you doing?" roars an enormous man as he strides into the clearing. "I'm Bombax, the owner of this circus and that pegasus. Leave her alone!"

"We're just petting her," you say.

"Don't you ever feed her?" Petra demands.

"Of course we feed her. But she won't eat. A waste of five thousand good gold pieces. I expect she'll die soon," the man says as he pokes the fragile pegasus with a fat finger.

"But you can't let her die!" you cry in horror. "Why don't you let her go?"

"NO! I bought her. She's mine! If she won't do as I want, let her die! I'll stuff her and put her in the sideshow! But that's my business, not yours. Get out of here and stop poking into things that don't concern you!" roars the man as you back away.

"Petra, we have to do something!"

"Like set her free?" asks Petra as you walk toward the brightly lit main tent.

"Do you think we could?" you whisper.

Backing into the shadows, Petra opens his hand. In his palm lies a silver key.

"Petra!" you cry, flinging your arms around him. "I'm always scared you'll get caught, but tonight I'm glad you can pick pockets. When should we do it? Now?"

"No. There are too many people around. Let's watch the show now. After it's over and everyone's gone, we'll free her."

"But, Petra, the longer we stay, the more trouble we'll be in when we get home."

"It's not our home!" spits Petra. "At your home, people love you, and no one loves us at the Drunken Crow. We'll get a beating when we go back, so let's make every minute count. Come on. Let's see the show." And grabbing your hand, Petra pulls you into the tent.

For a time, your loneliness and hunger vanish, erased by the magic of the circus. Only when the final trumpet blast fades do you stir from the hard wooden bench.

"Now, Petra?" you ask.

"Let's watch them take down the tent first. They'll be gone before morning. Wouldn't it be fun to go with them, always seeing new places and different people?"

"Hush, Petra. It scares me just to think about it," you say with a shiver.

Outside, a thick fog covers everything with a ghostly mantle. Huge figures loom out of the mist and tower above you.

"Mastodons," Petra says knowingly. "They pull up the pegs that hold the tent. Watch."

Outlined by the glow of flickering torches, the mammoth creatures lumber about, pulling pegs and poles and rolling up the tent. Then, over the trumpeting of the beasts, you hear the growl of thunder.

"Petra, it's going to storm."

"All the better for us." And as the first large drops of water begin to fall, Petra points to a red house wagon covered with gold designs. "We'll hide under there until everyone goes to sleep."

Scrambling under the wagon, the two of you settle down to wait. Soon you begin to nod drowsily. Hours later, you are wakened by heavy footsteps overhead.

"It went smoothly enough today," rumbles a gruff voice. "Now only four men stand between us and total control of Greyhawk."

"Can we do it?" a second voice asks nervously. "These people aren't stupid."

"Clusia, nothing can go wrong. No one knows except you, me, and the dopplegangers. All you have to do is get the next dopplegangers ready for tomorrow, and it will work like it always has. Two officials go into the fortune-teller's tent. Then—zippo, chango!—

out come two dopplegangers who look and act just like them but do as we command."

"I'm just worried, Bombax. I'd hate for anything to go wrong now."

"Nothing will go wrong. I'll see to that," the deep voice says menacingly. "I'll kill anyone who stands in my way."

"Come on, Laela. We've got to get out of here," whispers Petra as he crawls out from beneath the far side of the wagon.

Quickly the two of you dash through the pelting rain to the pegasus. You hug her wet, trembling body as Petra, with fumbling fingers, pushes the key into the lock.

"Hurry, Petra!" you call out as a mastodon begins to bugle an alarm.

"I'm trying! It's stuck!" cries Petra as a bolt of lightning rips across the sky.

As you cling to the quivering creature, a single tear flows down her muzzle. When you touch the tear with your finger, it turns to crystal and drops into your hand, where it lies like a shining star. Stunned, you look into the silver eyes of the pegasus.

"I will not forget," she whispers. "From this day forth, you are a part of me. When you need my protection or my presence, simply touch the tear or make a wish."

Another bolt of lightning explodes, and to your horror, you see the door of the red wagon swing open. A bellow of rage bursts from Bombax as he and Clusia, the ringmaster, struggle to get through the narrow doorway.

"Stop!" screams Bombax.

But it is too late. With a loud clanking, the lock opens and the chains drop.

"Fly! Fly away!" you shout.

"I shall not forget," promises the pegasus as she raises her feathery wings, lifts into the dripping night, and vanishes.

"Run, Laela!" cries Petra as he stumbles and slips on the muddy ground. But you stand statue-still, staring up into the empty sky. Then a heavy hand falls on your shoulder and spins you around—to face Bombax.

"You've just cost me a fortune, whelp!"

"I don't care! She's free now. You can't hurt her any more. No matter what you do to me, it was worth it!" you say defiantly.

"Leave her alone!" Petra screams as he hurls himself at Bombax and pounds the large body with his fists. Grabbing Petra with a huge hand, Bombax holds him at arm's length.

"Clusia, call the constable. We'll give him the boy, and they'll hang him."

Giving you a shove, he says, "Go home, girl. Just be glad I don't feed you to a monster."

"No," you say in a quiet but determined voice. "Let Petra go, or I'll tell."

Hissing, Bombax leans close to your face. "Tell? Tell what, girl?"

"We were under your wagon, and we heard everything. Let us both go, or we'll tell."

Tugging his tunic down over his bulging stomach, Bombax says calmly, "Clusia, find

14

someplace for our guests to spend the night—
someplace safe."

"Bombax, kill them! They'll ruin us!"

"Do as I tell you!" thunders Bombax, and
thrusting you and Petra into Clusia's arms, he
turns and strides away.

"I have to do everything," mutters Clusia as
he drags the two of you to a small, sturdy
wagon, shoves you inside, and locks the door.

"Laela, why did you tell them? Why didn't
you run when you had the chance?" groans
Petra from a dark corner.

"There wasn't anywhere to go, Petra. I
couldn't stand life at the Drunken Crow if you
weren't there. Besides, you got into this mess
only because of me. It's my fault we're here,"
you explain, and you begin to cry.

"It's not your fault, Laela. Don't cry."

Petra folds his arms around you until your
tears stop. "Get some sleep now. Everything
will look better in the morning."

Before falling into an uneasy slumber, you
carefully tie the crystal tear on a cord and
hang it around your neck.

During the night, you are wakened by the
cries of men and animals. The wagon suddenly lurches into motion, but its rhythmic
movement soon lulls you back to sleep. When
you waken again, daylight shines through
tiny cracks in the wall, and the wagon stands
motionless. Then the door swings open.

Standing in the bright sunlight, Bombax
glowers at you. "You have cost me five thou-

sand gold pieces and threatened me, but is Bombax angry? No! 'Why not?' you ask. Because Bombax is a fine fellow who loves everyone."

Wrapping one of his huge arms around your shoulders, he smiles thinly. "I'll make you a bargain. Join the circus. We're one big happy family, and you'll both like it here. We'll feed you, care for you, and teach you a trade. And you can work off your debt to me. Discuss it before I come back."

As Bombax relocks the door, you strain to hear what he is saying to Clusia on the steps outside. All you can make out are a few muffled words: ". . . don't care . . . decide . . . permanent accident. . . ."

Later, Bombax demands your decision.

"What would we do in the circus?" Petra asks warily.

1) "Since you like animals, you could learn to train them." Turn to page 47.

2) "You could learn to be trapeze artists." Turn to page 103.

3) "You could work with the sideshow." Turn to page 86.

No matter how desperately you cling to Petra, your hands continue to slip. With one last gesture, you clutch at the crystal tear that hangs from the cord about your neck.

As you slip from Petra's bloodless fingers and fall swiftly toward the waiting lurker, you wish with all your heart that the pegasus was near.

You feel a rush of wind and a sudden firmness beneath you, and looking down, you see a silvery back and two downy wings! Wrapping your arms firmly around the shining neck, you bury your face in the streaming mane and cry with happiness and relief.

Once, twice, three times the pegasus circles the tent, soaring and gliding like no bird since the beginning of time. Then she floats to earth and lands in center ring.

"Do you wish to stay?" she asks.

"Yes, I must," you answer.

"Then I bid you farewell. I shall not take the crystal, for this is an evil place, and you are not safe. My promise binds me more securely than the heaviest chain. Should you need me, I shall answer. Be well," whispers the pegasus and leaves in a flurry of feathers.

Thunderous applause erupts from the stunned audience. After a moment's pause, Clusia says, "There you have it, ladies and gentlemen! Laela and the Pegasus—an act you will see nowhere but at the Bombax Brothers' Circus! Let's have a hand for the little lady!"

Responding to the applause, you bow and curtsy. After a while you are able to escape into the cool night air and talk to Petra.

1) "Well, Laela, are you convinced now?" Petra demands angrily. "We were lucky this time, but Bombax will see to it that we don't escape again. I say we leave now, while we still have the chance!" Turn to page 148.

2) "Listen, Petra. That was my fault. I forgot to use the rosin. I still say we stay." Turn to page 32.

With tears blurring your sight, you turn and rush from the tent.

"Help! Help!" you cry as you run among the wagons.

"I suppose she'll find someone to help her—there's a do-gooder waiting behind every tree these days—but by then it'll be too late," chuckles Bombax as he and Clusia watch you from behind a brightly colored drum.

"This will cost us. Now we'll have to replace both Romney and the owlbear," mutters Clusia, gesturing toward the ever-weakening struggles beneath the net. "But at least we won't have to feed the lurker for another month."

"One more town and it won't matter what it costs," answers Bombax. "Now let's get out of here before the girl returns with help. It's best if everyone believes it was just an accident. And I don't think we need bother about the girl anymore. There's probably nothing she can do that will harm us."

THE END

"We'll start tonight," says Petra. "But you'll have to tell us what to do."

"First, we have to finish your makeup. Momo, you take Laela, and I'll do Petra." You change into full body tights, and under Momo's skillful fingers, every inch of you is plastered with the awful goop. Even your hair is tucked under a skintight cap that is covered with the makeup. As you peek in a mirror, your eyes blur with tears.

"Will I ever look normal again? Will it come off?" you whisper fearfully.

"Don't cry, dear," comforts Momo. "It's just a disguise that will come off with soap and water. And it may save your life. Now dry your eyes. The performance will start soon."

"Hey, Laela, isn't this neat!" exclaims Petra as he stomps out from behind a tree.

You're saved from answering by Helix leading you toward the midway.

"Now, remember—don't talk to people, but move enough so they know you're alive."

As you shuffle down the midway, you see Bombax standing beside a striped tent.

"That's the fortune-teller's tent," Helix whispers. "Don't do anything foolish. Follow my lead, no matter what I say. Remember that you're NOT Laela and Petra. You're living mummies and have been all your lives."

"Ah, there you are, Bombax," booms Helix cheerfully. "I've been looking for you. I want you to meet our new living mummies. They joined us a couple of days ago and will be

performing for the very first time tonight."

"Eh? What's that?' mutters Bombax, swiveling around to face you. "Living mummies, eh? Always a good draw for the suckers." His hard black eyes rake you, and you fear that he can see through your disguise.

Just as you are ready to turn and run, Bombax says to Helix, "What have you done with the two children I sent you earlier? I have plans for them."

"Children?" puzzles Helix, scratching his bald head. "What children?"

"The two chlildren!" Bombax repeats angrily. "The boy and girl I sent you, idiot!"

"I've seen no children, other than those from town," insists Helix. "Perhaps they'll show up later. I'll let you know if they do. Well, I'd best get these two started."

"WAIT!" snarls Bombax, placing himself in front of you. "What's your name?"

Your mouth grows dry. If you speak, Bombax will recognize you. You see Petra shuffle toward you. You have to act before he does something foolish.

1) If you want to try to bluff your way through, turn to page 123.

2) If you want to let Petra do something, turn to page 142.

3) If you are too scared to do anything but run away, turn to page 97.

"No! NO, your majesty! Don't listen to him. He's lying! He's trying to kill you. There are dopplegangers in the sideshow who will duplicate you. Don't go!" you yell.

"Heh, heh. The imagination of children. It's a wonderful thing, isn't it?" chuckles Bombax as he reaches down and pinches you.

"What's that you say, child? Speak up," commands the king.

"Don't worry yourself, your majesty," Bombax answers instead. "It's all the excitement, you know. The child will be fine after a nap—a very long nap. Why, there's no more truth to this silly story than saying I can fly."

No sooner are the words out of Bombax's mouth than one pegasus grabs the back of his collar and rises straight up into the air. Like a shadow, the second pegasus seizes Clusia and soars high into the air.

"Help! HELP! Don't let me fall!" screams Clusia. "I'll tell! I'll tell everything!"

"NO, Clusia! They're just bluffing!" hollers Bombax. "Keep quiet!"

Then, before your horrified eyes, the pegasi drop Bombax and Clusia. Down, down they plummet, with Clusia shrieking in fear.

"I'll tell! I'll tell!" he screams, and—so fast you are never certain you really saw it—both pegasi swoop down and catch the villains at the last possible instant.

Blubbering in terror, Bombax and Clusia vie to tell their tale of treachery.

"Well," says the king, stroking his beard.

"It seems that there is much more here than meets the eye. Guards, take these two away and lock them up someplace unpleasant until I have time to deal with them.

"Now, my young friends, that leaves you. Where are your parents, and what shall we do with you?"

"If you please, sir, we don't know who our parents are. We've never had any that we know of. We've always lived and worked at the Drunken Crow as servants—that is, until we ran away and joined the circus. But we don't want to go back there. We like it here. And we like learning how to be trapeze artists," Petra explains.

"But how can I leave you here with no one to look after you? You're too young to be out on your own," says the king.

"If you please, sir," interrupts Bebiana. "I wonder if I might do as a sort of guardian. Catcher and I would be pleased to say that they were part of our family. After all, we owe them our lives."

"Hmmm. Yes, I believe that would work out satisfactorily. Does that meet with your approval, children?"

Both of you gape at Bebiana.

As you fling yourself joyfully into his arms, you hear him say, "Of course, my name would still come first on the billing."

THE END

Looking around the tiny house wagon, you see a small, heavy stool and pick it up. Petra picks up a large wooden bucket and pours out the water. "Well," he says, "I hope this works." Then the two of you begin pounding on the walls and screaming as loud as you can.

You holler and bang for a long, long time. Finally, your hands grow sore and your voices roughen into hoarse whispers.

"What now, Petra?" you rasp.

"I don't know. I thought someone would hear us by now."

"We're pretty far away from everyone, and the noise from the circus is probably covering whatever noise we make," you gasp, your throat growing tight with strain.

"Let's try a little bit longer," whispers Petra.

At last, arms weak with exhaustion, you collapse in despair. You're sunk in gloom when a voice outside says, "What's going on in there? Is everything all right?"

You open your mouth to speak, but all that comes out is a hoarse croak.

"What's the matter, Anomura?" asks a second voice.

"I don't know. I was passing by, and I heard banging and pounding coming from this wagon. I hailed it, but there was no answer. I guess I was mistaken.

"Know where I can find some heavy rope? The number three line on the main tent snapped." The voices start to fade away.

Grabbing your stool, you leap to your feet

and start pounding frantically on the wall.

"Great starfish! There it is again! What is it? If someone's locked in there, why doesn't he say something?"

"I can explain, gentlemen," says a third voice. "That's my wagon. I've just purchased two monkeys that I hope to train to perform in the circus. No one answers you because there's no one inside but the monkeys."

"Well, I guess that explains it," says the first voice.

"Come on, Anomura. I'll help you find that rope," says the second voice.

Your last hope of rescue is fading fast. You must do something, or all will be lost. You have several choices:

1) Use the crystal tear and call the pegasus. Turn to page 36.

2) Rap on the wall in a pattern that no animal would use. Turn to page 93.

3) Give up and wait to see what happens. Turn to page 143.

While you stare in distress, Catcher swings faster, gaining height. With its long arms, the ape reaches for Bebiana.

Launched by a long drumroll, Bebiana flies through the air, tucks himself into a tight ball and turns four somersaults, then unfolds and is caught by Catcher.

"See, Laela? You were wrong. Nothing bad happened."

But you don't listen. Your eyes are still locked on Catcher. Instead of releasing Bebiana, the creature continues to grip him tightly.

Even the audience realizes something is wrong as Bebiana struggles in Catcher's grasp.

Suddenly, Catcher swings up onto the trapeze bar, dragging Bebiana along. The furry creature sits quietly for a moment, its eyes scanning the ground as though looking for something. You see its gaze find and lock on Bombax, who still stands hidden in the shadows. Something passes between the two—a look, a message, a spell.

Then Catcher emits a high, shrill, bone-chilling scream. Scooping up Bebiana, the animal flings him over one shoulder as though he were a rag doll and climbs up the trapeze to the very top of the tent.

"Catcher, come down!" you cry fearfully.

But Catcher keeps going toward the thin cables that crisscross the tent top. Leaping from the trapeze, the creature clings to one cable and inches its way outward.

Shrill screams reach your ears, and you see

Bebiana twisting in terror as he dangles from Catcher's shoulder, high above the arena.

Finally Catcher stops, clinging precariously to the thin ropes that stretch away from the highest point of the tent. For the first time, the powerful ape seems to realize exactly where it is. Wrapping muscular legs around the thin rope, Catcher looks downward for an instant, then covers both eyes and wails hysterically.

The audience gasps as Bebiana slips. For a long moment he dangles by his fingertips. Then, scrambling wildly, he claws his way up Catcher's body. Catcher screams and tries to shake Bebiana loose. Their bodies twist and turn, and you expect to see one or both plunge to his death. But miraculously, it doesn't happen, and both of them, aerialist and animal, cling desperately to the thin rope.

"Ten gold coins to the person who rescues them," yells the king.

1) "Petra, we have to do something. Let's try to get them down onto the trapeze." Turn to page 135.

2) "Bombax planned this," says Petra. "If we go up, we're as good as dead. I say it's time to leave." Turn to page 148.

3) "It's time to use the tear," Petra says. Turn to page 116.

Still clutching Petra's hand, you stand up as directed and walk slowly around the table toward the fortune-teller. When Petra starts to pull back, you look him straight in the eye and silently plead with him to follow your lead. He seems to understand, and turning, you approach the woman.

"Good. Just do as I say, and everything will be fine," says the fortune-teller.

As she reaches toward you, you lunge forward and shove the table at her. Caught off balance, the woman staggers and falls, and the table and cards tumble on top of her.

Quickly, before she can regain her footing, the two of you race out of the tent. Expecting an outcry, you zigzag in and out of the crowds that fill the midway and do not stop until you are safely inside Helix and Momo's wagon.

"Well, my goodness! What's the matter? You two look like you've just seen a ghost!" exclaims Momo as she enters the wagon, which sways from side to side under her great weight. You fling yourself into her arms, tears pouring down your face.

"Oh, Momo," you wail, "it was terrible! People looked at us like we were freaks, and the fortune-teller almost caught us, and—and I lost my candy."

"Hush, little one. Don't cry," croons Momo, rocking you back and forth. "Don't worry about people. Words can't hurt you."

"But, Momo, what about the fortune-teller?" asks Petra. "She must know about us."

"Ah, now that's another story. We'd best tell Helix and ask him what he thinks," says Momo.

"Hmmm. Maybe things aren't as bad as you think," says Helix as he furrows his brow in thought. "Oftentimes, things seem worse than they really are. I don't know Madame Leone. She never mixes with the rest of us. Could be she's as evil as Bombax, or maybe she's just a helpless pawn."

"But, Helix, she was trying to catch us," cries Petra.

"You don't really know that. Her actions could be viewed several ways. It's not good to judge without all the facts."

"So what should we do?" you ask.

1) "You could go back and ask her what she wanted." Turn to page 64.

2) "Or you could hide nearby and watch her for a while before you decide." Turn to page 133.

"Petra, how can we just run away?" you ask angrily as he pulls you out of the tent. "Romney's been good to us."

"I know. But there's no way we can save him, Laela. We'd be eaten ourselves.

"First the kamadan, now the owlbears. Bombax is trying to kill us. There's no way he's going to let us live. He just tricked us into thinking we were safe.

"Come on. We'll hide in the forest until the circus leaves, then make our way to a town."

"Hmmmm. Not quite what I had planned, Clusia," says Bombax as he steps out from behind the tent. "But it will do. Take the dopplegangers and go after them. Make sure they never come out of that forest. Too bad about Romney. Now I'll have to replace him as well as the owlbear.

"Ah, well. No one ever said circus life is easy."

THE END

Crabmen roustabouts scuttle around, taking down the big top, folding wooden seats, and packing props.

Stepping up to the nearest worker, you say, "Could you help us? We're with the circus now, and we have no place to sleep."

"Ask Anomura. He's in the center ring," the crabman answers.

Anomura dominates center ring, directing all the other workers. His body is large and well muscled, and his pincers and large, beaked nose look so scary that the two of you start to creep away without speaking.

"You there! Why are you sneaking about? Yes, you! Get over here! Hmmm. Aren't you the two who put the lurker to sleep?"

"Y-Yes, sir," you answer fearfully.

"Good! I admire courage. You'll have to tell me how you did it. That cursed lurker has eaten six of my men so far this season. Why are you here? Why aren't you sleeping?"

"Please, sir. We have nowhere to sleep. We were hoping you could help us."

"How about a trade? You tell me how you fixed the lurker, and I'll take care of you."

"That's fair," says Petra, and he explains how you put the lurker to sleep.

"Excellent," chuckles Anomura. "We have access to that wagon. Actually, I'd have put you up even if you hadn't told me. Anyone who angers Bombax is a friend of mine."

"Why do you work for him if you don't like him?" you ask.

"We don't work for him by choice," clacks the crabman. "Bombax raided our village four years ago and captured us. He took all the able-bodied crabmen away and left a party of sahuagins, seadevils, in control of our women and hatchlings. If we don't obey, word will be sent to the sahuagins, who will slaughter our families. So we continue to serve Bombax, but always we watch and wait. Our time will come," Anomura says bitterly.

"Maybe we can help each other," you say, and with a quick glance at Petra, you begin to tell your story.

"Shhh! There are too many unfriendly ears here," says Anomura. "Come with me."

Throwing open the door of a long, narrow wagon, Anomura motions you inside.

"Our accommodations won't suit you, but you may stay until morning. No one will harm you, and it's a safe place to talk."

Taking turns, you tell the crabman of Bombax and Clusia's plan to conquer Greyhawk.

"Such men are never satisfied with small worlds," says Anomura. "They must bring destruction to many before their hearts are glad. Does Bebiana know about this?"

"No! Why should he? All he's interested in is himself!" Petra exclaims angrily.

"Bebiana's a good man," says Anomura. "You just have to know how to talk to him. I think you should tell him.

"I'll leave you alone now, and I'll talk to my men. Perhaps, when the time comes, we may be able to help one another. Sleep well now."

As the door closes behind him, you stare about you curiously.

"I'm glad he's on our side," says Petra. "But I don't agree with him about Bebiana.

"Boy, it sure smells bad in here!"

"It smells fishy," you say, sniffing the damp, salty air that surrounds you.

"Where are we supposed to sleep?" demands Petra. "There's nothing here but these boxes filled with wet sand."

"It's where they sleep," you say.

"Ugh!" Petra shudders.

"If sleeping here will keep us alive," you say, crawling into one of the boxes, "we can stand it." And you make yourself as comfortable as possible for the night.

When you waken, the wagon is filled with rows of sleeping crabmen.

"Wake up, Petra. It's morning."

As you leave, you see Anomura lying on his side in the damp sand.

"Thank you," you whisper to him.

The crabman blinks a scaly eyelid, fans sand over himself, and sinks back into sleep.

As you emerge from Anomura's wagon shaking sand out of your clothes, Bebiana stomps up. "I've been looking all over for you!" he exclaims angrily. "We have to practice. My time is valuable, you know. I can't waste it looking for you every day."

Please turn to page 131.

You grasp the crystal tear and whisper, "Pegasus, please come to me." Almost before you have finished speaking, you hear delicate hoofbeats on the roof.

"What's that?" cries a startled voice.

"It's a pegasus!" the second voice yells. "Why's it pawing on that wagon? It acts like it wants to get in. Let's see what's inside."

"No! It's my wagon. I don't have to open it if I don't want to."

"I say open it," orders the voice of Anomura. "I can have a hundred armed crabmen here within two minutes."

"Bombax won't like this. You'll be sorry."

"Let me be the judge of that."

Then a key turns in the lock, and the door swings open.

"Monkeys, eh?" snarls a large crabman who stands in the doorway.

Then you are outside, breathing deeply of the sweet air. The pegasus flutters down beside you, and you hug her neck and bury your face in her shining coat. The creature nuzzles you gently and snuffles in your ear.

"Wait a minute!" snaps the crabman as he grasps the worker with a giant pincer. "Where do you think you're going? I think I'll hang on to you until we sort this thing out."

You hug Petra and the pegasus. Somehow you know that everything will be all right.

THE END

Later, in Romney's wagon, the trainer says, "I suggest you tell me what's going on before we all get killed."

"He's right, Petra. If we had confided in him sooner, Brutus might still be alive."

"We never meant for anyone to get hurt. We trusted him to do as he said," says Petra.

"Trusted whom?" asks Romney.

And soon the entire tale is told.

"I knew Bombax and Clusia were crooked, but this is incredible!" exclaims Romney.

"We've got to stop them," says Petra.

"Indeed, lad. And not just to save our own necks. He'll rape the land to satisfy his greed. Life won't be worth living."

"But what can we do?" you ask.

"I can think of several things," replies Romney with a grim smile. "My plan is dangerous, but it will work if you help."

"Just tell us what to do," says Petra.

"You'll have to perform tonight. The governor and the mayor of this province will be here, as well as Clusia and Bombax.

1) "We can get to the officials during the griffon act." Turn to page 149.

2) "We can use the cats and pray they obey us." Turn to page 84.

3) "We can use Caspius and hope we can control him." Turn to page 98.

"I think I'd like to walk around for a while and get used to things. It's all so different," you say.

"That's probably a good idea," says Momo. "Here, take some money with you and buy yourselves some treats."

"Just be sure you stay away from Bombax and Clusia and the fortune-teller's tent," warns Helix. "No sense looking for trouble."

"Don't worry, sir. We'll be all right," says Petra as you head for the midway.

Strange sights, sounds, smells, and colors swirl around you. Brightly colored tents line the midway. In front of each stands a costumed worker who readies himself for the first of the evening's customers.

Suddenly, the rich, mouth-watering aromas of cinnamon buns, boiled sweets, grilled meats, and roasted corn sweep over you.

"Let's buy some boiled sweets, Laela. I never get enough of them."

"We've eaten. We should save the money."

"Please, Laela. Please," begs Petra.

"Oh, all right. I guess it's OK."

Happily, the two of you hurry to the vendor and place your coins on the counter.

The seller pockets your money and hands you two sacks of the hot, sticky candy, then whispers, "Eat it somewhere else. The midway's opening. You'll scare my customers."

Only then do you notice what you have been too excited to observe before: People filtering onto the midway stop in shock at the sight of you, then quickly move out of your way. A girl your own age bumps into you, turns to apologize, then screams and buries her face in her father's chest.

"Get out of here!" hollers her father. "What are you doing out here with normal people? Get back where you belong, with the rest of the freaks!"

Your heart seems to shrivel within you. The sticky candy that tasted so wonderful only seconds before now tastes like sand.

Petra balls his fist and moves forward, but you put a hand on his arm and drag him into the nearest tent.

Darkness closes about you, and the cruel taunts fade from your ears. Petra puts his arms around you, and slowly the pain fades.

"Oh, how awful," you murmur. "Do you think people say things like that to Momo and Helix?"

"Of course they do," says a low voice. "But they got used to it. You will, too."

Heart pounding, you turn around swiftly but see nothing but darkness. Then a faint light appears in front of you. It grows larger and brighter until you can see the shadowy outline of a woman seated behind a draped table. You cannot see her face, for it is still too dark.

"Come, sit down. There is no need to be afraid of Madame Leone," says the gentle voice, as though reading your mind.

Mesmerized by her voice, you find yourself

moving forward, with Petra close behind. Silently, you seat yourselves on the chairs that stand before the table.

"Let me see what the future holds for you," says the woman as she spreads a deck of cards on the table in a smooth gesture.

Your breath catches in your throat as you gasp and clutch at Petra's hand.

The woman looks up from her cards, and a strange luminescence lights her face. Her large black eyes stare into your own, and you feel curiously empty—as though she knows your every thought.

"Ah, yes. I see. Now all is clear to me," she murmurs, rising from the table. Holding out her hands to you, she says, "I think it best that you come with me."

Your heart pounds in your chest, and you have a hard time breathing. You realize that you have accidentally stumbled into the fortune-teller's tent! You force your mind to think. You have two choices:

1) You can try to escape. Turn to page 29.

2) You can go with the fortune-teller and take your chances. Turn to page 56.

"Petra, tell me about lurkers."

"Well, they're tough and always hungry. They can be killed, but only if you have a weapon in your hand when you're attacked."

"What do they eat?"

"Anything that moves, and sometimes stuff that doesn't."

"Great! I think we might have a chance, Petra. They've got all kinds of dangerous animals here. They have to have some way of quieting them if they get out of control, probably some sort of potion that they use to catch animals in the wild. We have to find out where they keep that potion and then 'borrow' some."

Ten minutes later, with a wineskin taken from Bebiana's closet, the two of you crouch next to a small wagon marked AL-CHEMIST—NO ADMITTANCE.

"It's locked," you whisper.

"Leave that to me," says Petra as he melts into the shadows. Soon, you hear a faint click, and Petra whispers, "Come on!"

You enter the wagon and shut the door. Bundles of herbs hang from the ceiling, and bowls of strange substances that you are afraid to examine too closely fill the wall shelves. At the rear of the wagon is a large barrel bearing a sign that warns, DANGER! SLEEPING POTION! DO NOT BREATHE FUMES! DO NOT SWALLOW! DO NOT GET NEAR EYES! IF ACCIDENT OCCURS, GET VICTIM TO NEAREST HEALER!

Quickly you pry the top off the barrel. Trying not to inhale the fumes, you dip the wine-skin into the potent drug.

Holding the dripping bag away from you, you cork it, lower it to the floor, and cover the barrel.

"Whew!" gasps Petra as you back out of the wagon and run toward the big top. "My head was starting to swim. Let's hope this drug has the same effect on the lurker."

The two of you climb the ladder and squeeze onto one trapeze. Kicking higher and higher, you swing into position directly above the lurker and drop the bulging wineskin onto its upturned belly. Instantly, the lurker envelops the wineskin.

You stare in horror at the writhing gray mass below you. "That could have been one of us," you whisper numbly.

Then, even as you watch, the lurker sags to one side, slowly unfolds, and finally lies slack and still. The remains of the wineskin lie draped across it.

"Do you think anyone will notice?"

"I don't think so," Petra answers. "It looks the same. It's just not holding on to the poles. But it's too late to worry. The show starts soon, and we've got to get ready. We must have used enough potion to keep the lurker asleep for at least a few days."

Keeping that thought in mind, you race back to Bebiana's wagon and put on your costume. When the show begins, you're ready.

Although you're terrified at being so high

off the ground, you concentrate on all that you have learned, and soon you're standing on the platform with Bebiana, Petra, and Catcher, taking your first bow.

The four of you descend, only to be met at the foot of the ladder by a glowering Bombax.

"Hmmm. Something's upset our glorious leader," mutters Bebiana as he follows you out of the tent. "Whatever it is, I'm glad we aren't to blame."

Carefully avoiding Petra's glance, you do your best to stifle a giggle.

"Well," yawns Bebiana, "see you in the morning. Come on, Catcher."

"Where do we sleep?" you ask.

"How would I know?" Bebiana grumbles. "I'm not your baby-sitter. Here are your clothes. Take care of yourselves." And he enters his wagon and slams the door.

"Great. I guess we should have expected something like this!" Petra exclaims angrily.

"Don't worry. We'll find some place.

1) "We could sleep under the wagon." Turn to page 76.

2) "Let's sleep in the woods over there." Turn to page 141.

3) "Why don't we find out where the roustabouts sleep?" Turn to page 32.

You pile bedclothes around the bottom of the door, touch a candle flame to the heap, and watch as a sheet of fire shoots up. You begin to get scared.

"If the smoke gets bad, put this wet rag over your face and stay close to the floor. Heat rises," says Petra.

The two of you lie on the floor and watch the fire burn. Soon it begins to feed on the door. The air gets hot, and you worry that no one will see the blaze in time.

You're growing desperate when you hear the long-awaited cry of "FIRE!"

You and Petra crawl to your feet and, trying to stay away from the flames, pound on the walls and scream.

"There are kids inside!" cries a voice. "Here! Over here! Toss water on this wall! You! Get something to break down the door!"

At long last, an ax smashes through the wood. Within minutes, the door falls under repeated blows, and a crabman bursts in, scoops you up, and rushes outside.

"Oh, my poor babies!" cries a voice. Madame Leone rushes forward and, pulling you into her embrace, buries both of your faces in her bony chest. "Come with me. I'll take you home," she cries. And though you struggle mightily, you are unable to free yourselves.

"Just where are you going with my kids?" demands an angry voice. It's Momo!

"YOUR children? These are MY children!" insists the fortune-teller.

"Why don't we ask them," says Momo.

"Their minds are clouded with smoke," protests Madame Leone.

"Not that clouded," drawls Helix. "But if you don't let go of them, they may suffocate before they can tell us."

The fortune-teller's hands tighten, and colored spots dance in front of your eyes.

"Let them go," orders a deep voice, and the fortune-teller spins away from you.

You and Petra collapse onto the grass and gasp for air. When you're breathing more easily, you stand up and discover a large group of crabmen and other workers clustered around Madame Leone and the wagon's owner.

Over the protests of the woman and the worker, Helix is telling your story to the deep-voiced crabman.

"Seize Bombax and the others," the crabman commands his men. "Make sure that none of them escapes. It's time we put an end to this evil."

Struggling and fighting, Bombax, Clusia, and the last four dopplegangers are caught and thrust into sturdy cages.

"We'll bring them before the king and leave them to him. As for the children, where will they go?" asks the crabman.

"Home with our parents," you say, crossing over to Momo. "We've had enough excitement to last the rest of our lives."

THE END

"So you want to be animal trainers, do you?" Rebus Romney says doubtfully. "More likely you'll wind up as animal dinners. But you did let the pegasus go. That took courage."

"You're not mad at us for letting it go?"

"No, child. It needed to be done. The poor creature was grieving itself to death."

"Why didn't YOU let it go?" Petra asks.

Fixing his one good eye on Petra, the trainer rubs a calloused hand over his scarred face.

"Well might you ask," he sighs. "I cannot explain, boy. Just remember that none of us, people or animals, serves this circus by choice. Only death will free us.

"It isn't as bad for me as it is for the others, because I love my animals. But not all my animals feel the same about me."

"Are they all killers?" you ask.

"Most of them are. Come on. I'll introduce you. Remember," Romney says as you walk across the lot, "never give them a chance at you. Never trust them. You must be in control at all times, or they'll try to kill you."

Stopping before a large cage, he points inside. "Caterwauls. Never turn your back on one. They move so fast, you'll be dead before you hit the ground."

"But they look so nice!" you exclaim. "They have such beautiful blue fur."

"Aye, and those hooked ivory claws that can rip you to pieces—those are pretty, too. Look at the walls of the cage. Made of solid ironwood, but we have to replace it every few

weeks because they can claw through it."

"I bet I could work with them," claims Petra boldly.

"That's easy to say from this side of the bars," Romney replies as he walks on.

"Blink dogs! I like them!" you say. "And babies! May I pet one? Would it be safe?"

"Well, they're tamer than most, although we don't let on," says Romney as he unlocks the cage and reaches inside for a fat pup.

"There, there, Precious," he calms the mother. "We're just admiring your baby." Then he places the chubby pup in your arms.

"It's so soft. Oh, it's licking me! It likes me!" you cry joyfully.

Pushing her head between the bars, the mother dog grabs her pup, and instantly it disappears from your arms and reappears in the cage.

"That wasn't very nice, Precious. Laela was just petting Baby," scolds Romney.

"How do they do that?" asks Petra. "How do they disappear and reappear like that?"

"We don't know. It's just their way. They blink in and out, back and forth. One minute, they're in front of you; the next, they're six feet behind you. They growl and act vicious, which they can be. It makes a good act, and the audiences love it."

"Then what keeps them in?" you ask. "Why don't they all just leave?"

"The pups couldn't keep up, and the mothers won't leave them. Besides, I give them everything they need, even the chance to kill their enemies, displacer beasts. Blinks lose all sense when when it comes to these displacers."

Gesturing toward a heavily barred cage, Romney stares at the black, pantherlike creature that paces inside. It spits and hisses, and its green eyes, burning with hatred, watch the animal trainer's face.

Suddenly, a sharp-edged tentacle, one of two on the creature's back, lashes out and strikes the bars, inches from Romney's face.

"It's never stopped trying to kill me, and I don't suppose it ever will," he says. "Remember that. We breed them small, but even so, they're deadly—and deceptive, too. They always appear to be three feet from where they actually are."

"How do you keep them in?" you whisper.

"Magic. Bombax is an illusionist, you know. He keeps the spells up at all times, or I'd have been dead long ago, along with anyone else who stood in their path."

"How do you stay out of their way in the ring?" asks Petra.

"Practice. They're not very smart. I figure out what they're going to do, then move. It doesn't always work, of course. It was a displacer that hurt my eye."

"What's in there?" you ask, hurrying on to a large red cage.

"Owlbears. Both of you stay away from them, too."

"They don't look very mean," says Petra.

"They look silly, like someone glued owls'
faces onto bears."

"Silly, indeed! Just don't stick your hand
into that cage. We got these two as cubs. They
obey me most of the time, but they could kill
you easily if they felt like it."

Eyeing the savage beaks, the red-rimmed
eyes, and the long, sharp claws, the two of you
edge past the cage and follow Romney.

"Isn't there anything nice around here?"

"I've saved the best till last. Here they are,"
Romney says, parting a thicket of high grass.
"My pride of beauties!"

"Ohhh, Petra! Look! Griffons!" you say,
stopping short and sighing with pleasure.

Screeching loudly, the huge, winged, eagle-
headed creatures turn toward you. Powerful
muscles ripple on the lionlike hindquarters as
the griffons move closer.

"Show no fear," whispers Rebus Romney.

"They're beautiful," you say as you touch
the golden feathers of one animal. Its curved
beak hovers over your head, and its golden
eyes study you. Then the creature opens its
beak and issues a call. Instantly, all the griffons surround you, their enormous furred and
feathered bodies boxing you in.

"Laela!" screams Petra, rushing forward.

"Easy, lad. She's been accepted. I thought
they'd take to her. They'll not hurt her, but
what would you have done if they had? Griffons are fierce! Wild! They'd have ripped you
to shreds in seconds."

"I'd have stopped them! No bunch of birds is going to hurt Laela," mutters Petra.

"Come on, lad. Let's meet the 'birds,' as you so quaintly call them." Drawing Petra along, Romney pushes his way into the pack.

Although the trainer is accepted and Petra closely inspected, they are largely ignored as the griffons nuzzle and nudge you gently, each seeking your attention.

"Oh, Romney, they're gorgeous. Their feathers are beautiful, and their fur is so soft," you say, stroking each animal.

"Good girl. I thought they'd take to you. How would you like to ride them and learn to command them? It would be a great act."

"Could I really? Would they let me?"

"Yes. You have the gift, and I suspect Petra has it, too."

"What gift?" Petra asks suspiciously.

"The gift of caring, loving—whatever you want to call it. Animals recognize it and respect it. But if you don't have it, no amount of trying will get it. Of course, you must never use it unwisely. For example, you couldn't go into a kamadan's cage and expect the gift to protect you. And you must never betray an animal's trust.

"Well, that's enough for today. Why don't you two look around a bit. I'll see you at the lunch tent when the midday bell rings. Off with you now, and be careful!"

Assuring Romney that you will stay out of trouble, you and Petra wander among the brightly colored cages and wagons. Suddenly the air is filled with animal screams of rage and the cries of a person in pain.

"What can it be, Petra? It sounds as if someone's being killed. Where is everyone?"

"I don't know, Laela, but let's find out," says Petra as he dashes off.

The screams seem to be coming from behind a large green wagon. Cautiously you edge around it, then stop, frozen in terror.

Before you is a leopardlike kamadan, one of the most feared animals in the forests of Greyhawk. It measures a full eight feet from nose to tail, and snakes writhe on its shoulders. Clutched in its bloody jaws is the still struggling form of a crabman.

The kamadan drops the crabman and paces toward you. With its bloody fangs bared in a snarl and its awful orange eyes locked on yours, it slinks closer and closer.

1) "Run!" you gasp, yanking at Petra's hand. Turn to page 62.

2) "I'm not afraid! Romney says I have the gift! I'll take care of this!" says Petra. Turn to page 82.

3) "Cats love to chase things that run. Stand still!" you hiss. Turn to page 144.

You look questioningly at Petra.

"How can we find out where the rest of the dopplegangers are if we don't go with her?" he whispers urgently. "Either she's one of them and she leads us to them, or she's not and we've been worried about nothing. We'll be careful. We can always run."

"All right," you whisper back, "but we run at the first sign of trouble."

"Where are you taking us?" Petra asks the fortune-teller.

"All will be explained soon," she answers silkily, and motioning for you to follow, she leaves the tent.

The three of you wind through the midway until the crowds thin and you find yourself in a deserted area. Pits filled with roasting corn dot the ground. Madame Leone leads you to a wagon on the far edge of the pits. You notice worriedly that no one else is near.

Madame Leone knocks on the door of the house wagon, and it swings open. Smiling at you in a friendly manner, she waves you inside. As you step in, a terrible feeling of danger grips you.

Abruptly, the door slams shut, and Madame Leone turns a key in the lock.

"What's up?" says a deep voice. Turning, you see a worker seated at a heavy table.

"Find out for yourself," snaps the fortune-teller, and suddenly it feels as if a finger is stirring your brain.

"Hmmm! So these are the two Bombax told

us about. Good disguises. If I hadn't probed their minds, I'd never have known."

"What do we do now?" the fortune-teller asks harshly. "Take them over?"

"Can't," answers the worker. "There are only four of us left. Two take over the mayor and governor today, and two are for the king and queen. There aren't any of us to spare. We can lock them up here until it's all over tomorrow. Then we can dispose of them."

"What if others know of their existence?"

"No one's going to miss them. And even if they do, we just say we never saw them."

"A good plan," says Madame Leone. Then, roughly shoving you aside, she and the worker leave the wagon. You hear the turn of the key in the lock, followed by silence.

"Don't say it—I don't want to hear it," says Petra as he sinks to the floor.

"What are we going to do?" you ask.

1) "We could yell and bang on the door," suggests Petra. "Maybe someone would hear us." Turn to page 24.

2) "We could set fire to the wagon and hope that someone comes before we burn up," he says. Turn to page 45.

3) "We could just wait and hope Helix and Momo come looking for us," you say. Turn to page 143.

While you try to calm Caspius, Petra scoops up the net. Staggering under the weight of the enormous gray mass, he stumbles over the owlbear and drops the net over the animal's head.

Instantly, the roars cease. Reaching up with its front paws, the owlbear claws at the net, then finds itself caught fast.

"It worked, Laela. Stay there. I'm going to get Romney," Petra says as he tugs at the now-unconscious trainer.

As he grasps the animal trainer, an edge of the thick gray net falls over his hands. Ignoring it, Petra pulls at Romney, who still lies senseless across the owlbear. Somehow the net has spread itself across the unconscious man.

"Curse this net!" cries Petra as he attempts to brush it away.

"Laela, help! I'm stuck! The net—it's not a net! Laela, do something!"

1) If you are too afraid to do anything but run away, turn to page 18.

2) If you want to grab Rebus Romney's dagger and try to fight the 'net,' turn to page 71.

The two of you climb down from the stage and shuffle to the tent flap. You slip through it and walk into the darkness.

Years later, you and Petra sit in front of your wilderness cave and argue what you have argued a thousand times before.

"We should have stayed. We should have done something," Petra insists as he tosses another stick on the smoky fire.

"What could we have done?" you protest as you try to comb your long, matted hair with a pinecone. "The odds were against us. And from what we've seen over the years, I think we made the right choice. Bombax and his army of dopplegangers have practically enslaved the country. We were lucky to escape."

"But I don't want to be safe if I have to spend my whole life hiding in a forest. Besides, I miss Helix and Momo. Do you think they're all right?" Petra asks anxiously.

"Laela, why don't we leave here and try to find out what's happened?"

"It's too late," you say sadly.

"It's never too late!" cries Petra. "Come on, Laela. Say you'll do it. Say we can go," pleads Petra, seizing your hands.

Hope leaps within you for the first time in years.

"Yes, Petra, you're right. We'll track down the circus and find Helix and Momo. Somehow, we'll start over."

THE END

Using every muscle in your straining body, you haul yourself upward and cling to Petra's costume.

"Try to hold on a little longer," you pant between clenched teeth, while inch by agonizing inch, you pull yourself over Petra's body until you clutch the bar with your slippery hands. Trembling with the effort, you pull yourself up onto the bar and then help Petra up as well.

Only when the two of you are standing safely on the platform next to Bebiana and an excited Catcher does the audience respond, bursting into waves of thunderous applause.

"Bow!" hisses Bebiana. "Bow!"

You both bow shakily, then climb down the ladder as quickly as possible. Staggering with exhaustion, you make your way past the lurker and an enraged Bombax, and out into the cool night air.

1) "Laela, we've got to get out of here," Petra says. "That was just too close. Bombax's plan almost succeeded. I don't want to die, so let's leave while we still can." Turn to page 148.

2) "Petra, I forgot to use the rosin. It was my fault, not Bombax's. I think we should find a place to sleep tonight and stay." Turn to page 32.

Clasping Petra's hand, you turn and run from the fearful beast as fast as you can.

The kamadan utters a screech and pounces. Much like a cat plays with a mouse, it bats you and Petra along the ground. As you try to protect your face with your hands, you glimpse the crabman scuttling painfully away.

The snakes that sprout from the kamadan hiss and sway, each trying to sink its fangs into your flesh. Growling ferociously, the kamadan crouches over the two of you and breathes into your frightened faces.

Instantly, your eyes close and you sleep.

Hours later, you waken slowly and find yourself in a bunk in Romney's wagon.

"If this is how you keep out of trouble, I don't want to see how you get IN trouble!" grumbles Romney.

"It was an accident, sir," Petra mumbles groggily. "What happened?"

"It was horrible," you sob. "I thought it was going to eat me."

"It would have, too, if the crabman hadn't found me. Fortunately, it breathed a sleep spell on you. If you had fought, you'd be dead now. Frankly, I'm surprised you survived the spell."

"Why didn't it hurt you?" asks Petra.

"I'm immune to the sleep spell, and the snakes aren't poisonous. All I have to look out for are its fangs and claws. And I have a few tricks of my own. You two were lucky this time. Next time, you might not be."

"How did it get out?" you ask.

"That's the question, lass. The first rule around here is never to leave a cage unlocked. The lock and chain from that cage were on the ground. It might have been an accident, or just meant to look like one. So I tell you again—be careful!

"It's time for the evening performance. I want the two of you to lie down and rest and stay in this wagon until I get back!"

Grabbing his whip, Romney steps out and slams the door behind him.

Dimly you hear the roars of animals and the happy shrieks of children.

"Petra, I think Bombax tried to kill us. That kamadan didn't get loose by accident."

"Maybe Romney's part of it," Petra says blackly. "Maybe HE wants us dead, too."

"I don't believe that," you say. "After all, he rescued us. He's our friend, and I think we should tell him what's happening."

"We don't have any friends," says Petra. "We can't trust anyone except ourselves. We've got to get away from here."

"But, Petra, Rebus Romney said to stay here. I think we should do what he says."

1) "We can't trust ANYONE," insists Petra. "Let's leave." Turn to page 139.

2) "I think we should stay," you say. Turn to page 127.

"This is crazy," grumbles Petra. "We know she's involved with Bombax. Talking to her is like sticking your head in a lion's den and asking the lion if it's hungry."

"Possibly," agrees Helix, "but won't you feel better if you know for sure?"

"Won't do me any good if I'm dead, or if a doppleganger has my body," mutters Petra.

"Here we are," says Helix, and he sweeps the tent flap aside and ushers you in.

A shadowy figure stirs in the darkness. "You wish your fortunes told?" whispers a voice, and a soft glow fills the air.

Before you stands the fortune-teller, but something is different. Earlier, she seemed friendly. Now she seems hard and cruel, and evil seems to flow out of her toward you.

"We thought you might tell my friends what the future holds," Helix says calmly.

"And what if they have no futures?"

"No futures?" you gasp.

Madame Leone's voice changes, and she laughs softly. "Just a little joke," she says.

"Not very funny," growls Petra. "Come on, Laela. Let's go."

"Wait," drawls Helix as he leans against a tent pole and stuffs his pipe with tobacco. "If you won't tell them their fortunes, tell them what it's like to be a doppleganger."

Madame Leone draws back in shock.

"A doppleganger? What are you saying? How would I know what it's like?"

"We know all about the plot," yells Petra

angrily. "You're not fooling us, not one bit."

Then, even as you watch, Madame Leone's figure wavers like a painting blurred with water. It seems to fade away, and standing in its place is something horrible to behold. A skeletal figure covered with folds of loose gray skin starts slowly toward you, its red eyes gleaming crazily.

"Run, Helix!" you shout, and turn to flee.

"Nope. This circus is my home, and I'm not letting an ugly, shape-changing monster ruin it for me. Why, it could give circuses a bad name," drawls Helix. "You two step outside and yell 'Hey, rube!' as loud as you can. As soon as help arrives, show 'em in."

"You think your silly circus traditions can save you? You are stupid, human. Nothing will save this circus, and you are as good as dead," sneers the doppleganger, advancing on Helix. "You cannot fight me."

"We'll see about that," says Helix as he carefully extinguishes his pipe. Then he springs at the doppleganger.

You and Petra race outside and scream "HEY, RUBE!" as loud as you can.

Almost immediately, you are surrounded by a huge crowd. Everyone holds a weapon.

"Hurry! There's a doppleganger inside trying to kill Helix!" you yell.

"Helix? Let's go!" shouts a crabman, thumping an iron rod against his pincers.

"No! Wait! There are no dopplegangers in my circus! Everyone get back to work!" cries

Bombax as he pushes urgently through the crowd.

The crowd pauses, then surges forward.

"Take one more step, and none of you will have jobs!" yells Bombax.

"Jobs? No—slave labor!" screams a large crabman, clacking his pincers excitedly.

The mob shouts in agreement, and you fear that fighting will break out before Helix is rescued. Then the tent flap opens, and silence falls. Helix stands in the doorway, his body twisted around the snarling doppleganger.

"No need to rescue me," drawls Helix. "This fellow isn't as tough as I thought."

The doppleganger shrieks in rage and struggles to free itself, and Helix twitches. His long arms, legs, and body tighten around the monster, cutting off its cries.

"They don't call me 'Double Helix, the Amazing Stretching Man' for nothing. Now, just so you folks didn't show up for no reason, Laela and Petra are going to tell you a story. Won't take long, and I think you'll find it real interesting. And, Anomura, why don't you stay near our friend Bombax."

Nervously, you and Petra tell your story.

Cries of outrage greet your words, and Bombax struggles in the crabman's claws.

"Where are the other dopplegangers?" asks Anomura, clicking a claw under Bombax's nose.

"What others?" blusters Bombax.

SNIP! Half of Bombax's mustache falls to

the ground. "Mustaches grow back. Noses don't," says Anomura as Bombax blubbers in fear.

"They're working as corn vendors!"

Waving his claw in an abrupt gesture, Anomura disperses his fellow crabmen to search for the rest of the dopplegangers, then turns to Helix. "What about these two?"

"Put them together in a closed wagon and lock the door. We'll deal with them later."

"No! You can't put us together. It'll take me over! It'll kill me!" screams Bombax.

"You should have thought of that before you started all of this," drawls Helix.

"Please don't put us together," pleads Bombax. "If you keep it away from me, I'll do anything you want!"

"Will you tell the king where all the dopplegangers are in the other towns?"

"Yes! Yes! Anything!" sobs Bombax.

"That sounds fair, doesn't it?" you ask.

"Sure does. Can't have them roaming around the country. But now I think you should get back to the wagon. Your mother will be worried about you," says Helix."

"Our mother?" questions Petra.

"That's what I said. Unless you two figure you're too old to have parents."

"Oh, no. We're not too old, are we, Petra?"

Petra smiles at you, and you know that, at last, you're home.

THE END

"I like it here, in spite of Bombax. He may think he can kill us like flies, but we'll prove him wrong," you say angrily.

For the rest of the afternoon, you and Petra practice as though your lives depend upon it, which indeed they do.

By evening, you are nearly exhausted, but you feel a new confidence. You barely have time to change into your costume before you hear the music introducing your act, and you and Petra race breathlessly to the tent.

"And now Bombax Brothers' Circus introduces Laela and Petra, the world's youngest trapeze artists, performing for your pleasure, high above the circus floor. Note that they are performing without a safety net. Should they fall, all that will prevent them from injury is the lurker above, which has spread itself below the trapeze rigging."

As you hurry to the ladder, Clusia points out the lurker. The audience gasps, and the ringmaster continues. "No one has fallen in recent years, but you never know . . . ."

You step hesitantly onto your trapeze and begin to swing back and forth, picking up speed rapidly. The light from torches high on the tent poles illuminates your every move and nearly blinds you. All your practicing seems very long ago, and you wonder what you are doing in this scary place where people are trying to kill you.

"Laela!" Petra yells. "Snap out of it! Come on. It's time."

You take several deep breaths to calm your pounding heart, get a firm grip, and begin to pump with your legs. Higher and higher you swing, finally brushing the tent top with your toes. Then you drop backward, grasping the bar under your knees.

Faster and faster you swing, gauging your timing exactly. Then you let go and fly through the air like a graceful bird. Hands outstretched, you soar straight toward a waiting Petra, and relief pours through you as you grab his wrists.

However, a sudden surge of terror strikes you when you feel your hands slip. Slowly, so slowly, your sweaty hands slide down Petra's wrists, your own weight pulling you down toward the lurker—and death.

"Petra, I'm slipping! Help me!"

"I can't," Petra gasps as he hangs upside down. "I'm slowing down. You're a dead-weight."

You realize that you must do something, or you'll fall and make Petra fall, too.

1) You can let go and hope that you can avoid the lurker. Turn to page 147.

2) You can hang on and hope for help. Turn to page 60.

3) You can grab the crystal tear and call the pegasus. Turn to page 16.

Without a second's hesitation, you rush to the fallen trainer and snatch his dagger.

Circling the edges of the gray mass that has now almost entirely engulfed Petra, you plunge the knife into its center. Instantly, the "net" shivers and utters a thin cry.

Doing your best to avoid Petra and the owl-bear, you strike the deceptive monster again and again with the sharp blade.

At last, emitting a quivering wail, the monster twitches and collapses.

Quickly you tug at Petra's hand, all that remains outside the blob. Even in death, the monster is reluctant to give up its victims, and only with difficulty are you able to free your friend.

Wheezing painfully and holding his aching head, Petra sits up slowly.

"Get up, Petra. You've got to help me get the others out, or they'll die."

"We ought to let the owlbear," mutters Petra. "This is all its fault." But staggering to his feet, he helps you move the gray blob and free Romney from Brutus's grip.

"No bones broken," says Petra, running his hands over the trainer's body. "Probably just half-squashed." And leaning forward, he breathes gently into Romney's mouth.

Seconds later, Romney draws a long, shaky breath and opens his eyes. As color returns to his pale face, he gasps, "What happened?"

"Brutus grabbed you," says Petra, helping Romney up. "Then I used that net, but it came

to life and tried to eat us. It almost did, too, but Laela killed it."

"I used your dagger," you say. "I didn't know what else to do."

"You did well, lass. That's a lurker above, not a net, but Bombax uses it as a net for the trapeze act. If anyone falls, the lurker has dinner. I should have warned you. I just never expected you would need to know so soon.

"But what I don't understand is what came over Brutus. I can usually trust my owlbears." Bending over the still form, Romney inspects his animal.

"It's dead," he says sadly.

"Dead? Why? We got it out!" you cry. "It couldn't have suffocated so quickly!"

"I expect we'll find it was poisoned," Romney says, his face twisted with grief.

"But why? Who would do such a thing?" Petra asks angrily.

"I don't know, but I'm going to find out. I raised Brutus from a cub. I'll miss him sorely," Romney answers bitterly.

Suddenly, a great roar splits the air as Caspius shuffles over and sniffs at Brutus. Then a wheezy wail bursts from its throat.

You hug its great furry body and say, "Don't cry, Caspius. We'll catch whoever did this. Hush. Everything will be all right." And slowly you lead the grieving bear away.

Please turn to page 37.

"Here we are," says Helix, pointing to a blue and white tent with a banner that reads, SEE THE AMAZING LIVING MUMMIES. Inside are a small stage and two chairs.

"I don't think I'm going to like this."

"Don't be a spoilsport, Laela. It'll be fun. Pretend it's Fright Night and we're in costume." Petra turns to Helix. "We never got to do that. We always had to work."

Remembering your life at the Drunken Crow is enough to make you climb up on the stage and sit next to Petra on the small chairs.

Soon people begin to wander among the brightly colored tents, and Helix cries, "Hurry! Hurry! Hurry! Step inside and see the amazing living mummies. Alive for thousands of years in a mummified state, yet as human as you or I! Hurry! Hurry! Hurry! Only one coin to see the living mummies!"

The hours creep by as people gape at you with big eyes and open mouths. Just when you feel that you can't stand one more second of the horrible pretense, Helix enters.

"Good work, kids. People loved you. Relax awhile, now—the show's started. I'm going to the wagon to get us something to drink. I'll be right back."

"Wow, Laela, that was fun!" Petra says. "I love being a mummy!"

You are about to reply when Bombax, Clusia, and a veiled woman enter the tent.

"Here they are. Horrible, aren't they?" says Bombax, gesturing toward you. "They'll do admirably. It's lucky we found out that the king doesn't believe in fortune-tellers. It could have ruined all our plans."

"How can these two ugly creatures help us?" asks the fortune-teller.

"The dopplegangers will take over these two mummies," says Bombax. "Then tomorrow, we'll bring the king and queen here, and the mummies—or rather the dopplegangers in their bodies—will take over them. It's simple."

Suddenly, the fortune-teller looks up, and her eyes meet yours.

"What about them? They think and feel, and they've heard your plan. Do you not fear that they will object to being done away with?" asks the fortune-teller.

"Them?" scoffs Bombax. "They're too dumb to understand what we're saying. Let's get the dopplegangers. There's still much to be done."

As the tent flap drops, Petra jumps to his feet. "Come on, Laela. We've got to leave here, or they'll get us."

"But what can we do, Petra?"

1) "Tell Helix. He'll know what to do." Turn to page 83.

2) "Use the crystal tear." Turn to page 140.

3) "Run for it. There's no way we can win." Turn to page 59.

"This is fine," you say, crawling wearily under the wagon. "They'll be packing up the show soon anyway, so let's just sleep here till then. I'm so tired, I've got to get some rest." And pulling your long, heavy skirt around you, you curl into a ball and settle down for the night.

"I don't think this is a good idea," mutters Petra as he stares into the shadows. "I'm tired, too, but I'm going to stay awake in case Bombax shows up."

Petra stands defiantly in front of your curled figure, but as the hours pass with no sign of danger, his eyes grow heavy with sleep.

At last he sinks to the ground and rests his head upon his knees, fighting to stay awake. His eyelids blink once, twice, and slowly close. Finally, sleep claims him.

"Excellent!" says a voice that half-wakens you and that your sleepy mind recognizes as Bombax's. Forcing your heavy eyelids open a fraction of an inch, you see Bombax stepping out from behind a tree. Chuckling, he rubs his hands together briskly and says, "Clusia, tell our friends to come along. It's time for them to go to work."

Groggily, you try to focus your weary eyes as two large, shadowy figures step from the woods and creep forward.

"There are your new bodies," Bombax says, pointing toward you and Petra. "I expected you two to replace the king and queen, but these two are just as important—they could ruin all my plans. So take them over, and later, when it's safe, we'll change you into more suitable beings."

All of your senses scream in warning as the two shadowy dopplegangers flit forward like fog and hover over you and Petra. You open your mouth wide to scream for help, but no sound emerges. An icy deadness fills your mind and paralyzes your body. You are helpless.

Dimly, you're aware of Bombax's voice.

"Well, Clusia, a good night's work after all," he rumbles as he stares at the replacement process going on. "Tomorrow, and for as long as we wish, these 'children' will do exactly as we want. Then, when it is totally safe, we can get rid of them.

"How very nice of them to let us catch them so easily. How nice indeed!"

Slowly, like sand trickling through an hourglass, the shadowy figure above you seems to melt away, and you feel a pressure building inside you. To your horrified mind, it seems that your body and soul are fighting a losing battle against an invisible invader. Then, with one last burst of resistance still struggling within you, you know no more.

THE END

"OK, Helix, we'll be living mummies," you say. "What do we have to do?"

"Do you want to start tonight? You can if you want to, or if you'd rather, you can get completely made up and then just walk around awhile and get used to things," says Helix.

1) If you want to start right away, turn to page 19.

2) If you want to explore for a while, turn to page 38.

As the bright stars start to fade into a gray dawn, you and Petra slip onto the backs of two pegasi. Perched on the lip of the nest, your steed stretches his immense wings and glides into the wind.

Higher and higher you fly, until you feel that your heart, mind, and body are becoming part of the sky.

Fear fades as you grip the pegasus with your knees. With a feeling of great joy, you open your arms and lean into the wild wind.

When at last your pegasus returns to the nest, all thoughts of the circus and of man have vanished. You are at peace. You are as one with the pegasus.

THE END

"Well, I have the gift, too. Rebus Romney said so. I should be part of this," you say, grabbing a branch off the ground.

Snatching the heavy door chain from the ground, Petra advances slowly.

"YAAHH!" he yells, waving the chain in the kamadan's face. "Get back in the cage, cat. I'm not afraid of you! YAAHH!"

The kamadan roars and springs, and your world becomes a wild whirl of fur and fighting.

Later, the big cat crawls back into its cage and grooms itself, purring contentedly.

"Well, Clusia," says Bombax as he chains and locks the cage, "I'd say your plan worked out quite well. Quite well indeed."

THE END

Moving as quickly as your mummified feet will allow, you head toward the wagon. "Helix! Momo!" you cry through stiff lips.

As you near the wagons, you hear footsteps behind you. Turning awkwardly, you see Bombax, Clusia, Madame Leone, and two others running after you.

"Stop them!" Bombax calls harshly. "We can't allow them to get away!"

"Run, Laela!" gasps Petra. "I'll try to stall them. Get help."

Panic-stricken, you shuffle into the camp and cry, "Helix! Momo! Help!"

But no one answers. You stare at the deserted camp and realize that no one is there. There's no one to depend on but yourself. Somehow you must help Petra. Possibilities race through your mind. You can

1) Try to rescue Petra yourself. Turn to page 157.

2) Go for help. Turn to page 106.

As the evening show starts, the cats shift restlessly on their gaily painted drums, tentacles waving wildly and fangs glinting in the bright lights.

"They seem disturbed tonight," observes Romney. "I suppose they're picking up our vibrations. They can do that, you know. If you become nervous, they will know it instantly. If you feel fear, they will sense it, and it could mean your death.

"Never forget how quickly they move. Should they attack, they would move too fast for me to be able to rescue you. Once we enter the cage, you're on your own. Do you still want to go through with it?"

"We're not afraid. We have the gift—you said so yourself," Petra says bravely.

You start to protest, then realize that unless you perform, the kingdom could be lost to the evil Bombax. So you say nothing.

Squaring your shoulders, you step inside the metal cage in the center ring. Petra and Romney follow you, and the door clangs shut.

A drumroll signals the start of the act. Then a high, shrill, ear-piercing melody winds its way into the cage.

"Stop that!" screams Romney, turning from one direction to the other in a frantic attempt to find the source of the music.

But the dreadful, shrill music doesn't stop. It sends shivers up your back, and it drills into your head. You sink to the ground and cover your ears with your hands, trying desperately to shut out the fiendish notes that seem to vibrate within your very being.

Through tear-filled eyes, you see Romney attempting to control the cats, who writhe in anguish as the terrible noise plays upon their delicate senses. Roaring in pain, the kamadans leap from their drums and lash out at the only visible enemy—YOU.

Howling horribly, the caterwauls shake their black-maned heads, crawl down from their pedestals, and begin to slink toward the three of you. You know that if you are to live, you must get out of the cage.

"Petra!" you cry feebly. "Crawl to the cage door. We've got to get out of here, or they'll kill us."

Cracking his whip, Romney joins you. The three of you inch your way among the crazed cats as they stalk you and circle you, slashing and clawing at the air as they move.

With great care, the three of you weave your way to the cage door. Romney reaches up and tugs, but the door doesn't open.

"Romney, it's locked," whispers Petra, pointing to a chain encircling the iron bars.

You are vaguely aware of the screaming crowd, the advancing cats, and the satisfied smile on Bombax's face as everything starts to spin around you, and you wonder faintly if this is . . .

THE END

That afternoon at the sideshow, a gaunt man runs a hand over his skeletal head, looks at you with large brown eyes, and says gently, "No need to be afraid, little ones. I won't hurt you." Incredibly tall and thin, with long, thin arms and legs, he looks more like a starved stork than a man.

"Piffle, Helix! You're not gong to convince them just by telling 'em so. They'll have to learn that for themselves,' says an immensely fat and friendly-looking woman.

"Now, now, babies. Don't you worry about a thing," she says, gathering you both to her enormous bosom. As she enfolds you in a hug, she adds, "You're safe with Momo and Helix."

"We're NOT babies!" Petra says hotly, squirming out of her embrace.

"Well, my dears, we mean no offense. It's just that Helix and I have no children of our own. It's a grief to us.

"If you'd care to join us, I've got a nice pot of soup on the fire and some sweet buns ready to come out of the oven."

"Yes, ma'am!" Petra cries eagerly.

Shyly you sit down next to the odd couple and eat the best meal of your life.

"Forgive us if we've been rude," you apologize, "but most people aren't so nice to us."

"And don't we know it, little lamb. Don't we just know it," sighs Momo, hugging you.

"Helix and I aren't quite what folks on the 'outside' consider normal. So they don't take too much care being nice to us, either."

"You? There's nothing wrong with you," Petra says, slurping his soup noisily.

"We know that," Momo laughs, "but other folks don't think so. Why, they take one look at this husband of mine, and that's it. They can't take him seriously—and him with a lawyer's training and a fine, sharp mind. We almost starved when he set up office. And when they see us coming down the street together, you should hear them laugh.

"It's not as though I can help being so short and so fat. I pray to all the gods, but I just keep getting bigger," sniffs Momo.

"Don't worry about what others think, Mother," Helix says, patting her broad back.

"Do people really laugh at you?" you ask.

"Of course they do. We're different, Momo and I. Oh, we're not REALLY different, only in the way we look on the outside. But most folks don't look any further. Being around someone who's different makes people angry because it forces them to realize that they may be less than perfect themselves.

"So Mother and I decided to join the circus. Here we're normal. No one looks at us funny or says things to hurt us."

"No one except the townies we see every day. They still poke fun at us!" cries Momo.

"Now, Mother, they don't know any better. You just have to ignore them."

"I'm sorry if we hurt your feelings," you say. "Everything has happened so fast, and we don't know whom we can trust around here.

"Thank you for feeding us. It was the nicest meal we've ever had, and Petra and I would be pleased if you'd be our friends."

"Perhaps you better tell us why you're here," Helix says, stretching out his great length and lighting his pipe with an ember.

You and Petra look at each other, and a wordless decision passes between you. In a very short time, you have told your story. Then a long silence falls, broken only by the crackling of the fire.

"I always knew there was something funny going on here, but I just closed my mind to it," says Helix. "Are you quite sure about the dopplegangers and the fortune-teller?"

"Absolutely!" you declare.

"Well, Mother, we shall have to do something," Helix says. "This is our home, and we're loyal subjects of Greyhawk. If Bombax has his way, he'll destroy our lives in his search for power."

"Oh, Helix, where will we go? What will we do?" Momo wails hysterically.

"Don't worry, Mother. Everything'll be all right. Leave it to me."

"Can we help?" asks Petra. "This means a lot to us, too. We have nowhere else to go."

"It might well be dangerous," says Helix. "Bombax and Clusia aren't stupid."

"If they can be stopped, we want to help."

"All right," says Helix. "But the two of you will definitely have to disappear now."

"I'm not going to hide," Petra growls.

"I was thinking of disguising you, not hiding you," Helix explains.

"What do you mean?" you ask.

"Become part of the show. Bombax would look right at you and not even see you."

"What would we do?" you ask, both doubtful and curious.

"You could be living mummies."

"Would it hurt?" asks Petra.

"Of course not. It's just makeup. Here, I'll show you. I'll do your hands and faces, and you can see what I'm talking about," says Helix as he rummages through a large box.

"Do living mummies really exist?" you ask, sitting at his feet.

"Well, yes and no," answers Helix as he opens a large can. "Sometimes people get an illness that makes their skin shrivel. The cause is unknown, and there's no cure. When it dries, this makeup will make you look just like those people," he says as he spreads an icky goop on your face.

"The act is simple—you just move around a little and let people look at you so they know you're alive. Sometimes they talk to you. I suggest you pretend you can't speak."

"UGH! You look horrible, Laela!" exclaims Petra. "If I didn't know it was you, I'd be scared to death."

You hold up your hands and stare at them in horror. Your skin is now gray-green, wrinkled, and dead-looking. Even though you know it's only makeup, you're frightened.

"Now it's your turn, lad," says Helix.

Amazed, you watch your friend turn into a thing of horror. Noticing your look, Petra claws at you with his awful hands.

Even though you know it's Petra, you shriek in terror and hide behind Momo.

From behind her skirt, you see a crabman roustabout appear and sidle up to Helix.

"Have you seen two little kids, Helix?"

"No, I don't believe I have. Why?"

"Heard Bombax whispering to that rat-faced Clusia about getting rid of them. Sounded like he meant forever. Thought I'd try to find 'em and warn 'em." Then, noticing you for the first time, he adds, "I thought your living mummy quit the show."

"So she did," drawls Helix. "But we were lucky enough to pick up these two a couple of towns back. They haven't exhibited yet—too shy. Need to get used to people looking at them. We'll probably show them tomorrow."

"You better. You know how Bombax is about feeding people who don't work."

After the crabman leaves, Petra says, "He seemed nice. Why didn't you tell him who we really are?"

"The fewer people who know who you are, the safer you'll be," answers Helix. "Now it's almost time for the evening performance. Are you going to join us or not?"

"Can Laela and I talk for just a minute?"

"Of course," replies Helix. "Come along, Mother. Let's leave them for a while."

"Oh, Petra, what should we do? This disguise would work, but it's so creepy."

"Well, our choices are clear," says Petra as he admires his mummy hands.

1) "We can be living mummies in the sideshow." Turn to page 78.

2) "We can go back and be animal trainers." Turn to page 47.

3) "Or we can be trapeze artists." Turn to page 103.

Carefully, you rap on the wall in a specific rhythm. One. Pause. One, two. Pause. One, two, three. Pause. One, two . . .

"That's no monkey!" cries the crabman. "Open that door, or I'll break it down!"

"If you know what's good for you, you won't mess with me and what's in that wagon. Bombax won't like it," snarls the worker.

"Oh-ho, Bombax is behind this, is he? In that case, I INSIST you open the door."

Then there is a cry of pain, and seconds later, the door swings open.

You and Petra stumble out and stand in a daze, nearly blinded by the bright torches.

"Why, it's a pair of living mummies!" exclaims one of the crabmen.

Frantically, you start to peel the makeup from your face. Petra helps you, and soon your features emerge from the awful disguise. Then, straining your throat, you rasp out the words, "Helix . . . Momo."

"Helix and Momo? OK, kids. I can't—oh, no, you don't, fella," says the crabman as he seizes the worker in his large pincer. "You've got some explaining to do."

As the five of you start walking toward Helix and Momo's wagon, you're joined by more and more crabmen, until you're surrounded by a clacking red army. You link arms with Petra and smile happily. You know that everything will turn out well.

THE END

Quickly, you draw forth the precious crystal tear that hangs about your neck. Fearfully, you approach the enraged owlbear.

Howling hideously, the owlbear drops Romney and charges toward you. With its eyes gleaming wildly and its sharp beak clacking noisily, the owlbear encircles you with its deadly claws.

Petra leaps on the owlbear and rains a flurry of blows upon its broad back. "Let go!" he screams, yanking fur and feathers.

Suddenly, the animal's screams are replaced by a rumbling that is almost a purr.

Held fast by the thick, furry forearms of the owlbear, you look into its eyes and smile. You touch the crystal tear and wish hard, then pat Brutus gently.

"Good Brutus," you murmur. "Put me down. That's right. Now tell us what's the matter."

Scrambling down from the creature's back, Petra stands beside Romney, who runs skilled hands over the huge beast. When he touches Brutus's stomach, the owlbear roars in pain.

"Poison. We've got to give it an antidote or it'll die. You two stay here. Try to keep it quiet. I'll be right back," says Romney as he races from the tent.

By the time Romney returns, Brutus lies curled in a tight ball on the ground, breathing with difficulty. You sit by the animal's side, holding one large paw.

Prying open the sharp beak, Romney pours a thick green fluid down Brutus's throat.

"This might work. Without knowing what manner of poison it was, I can't be sure.

"You two get back to the wagon and wait for me. I'm going to stay here till Brutus is out of danger. Take good care of that crystal amulet, Laela. It's lucky for us that you had it."

Reluctantly, the two of you leave.

"Petra, stop. My legs are trembling so much I can hardly walk," you say as you collapse on the steps of a nearby wagon.

"I was so scared," you admit shakily. "I thought Brutus was going to kill me."

"But it didn't happen. You're alive. And there's nothing wrong with being scared. It WAS scary. The thing is, you acted even though you were frightened. I don't know if I could have. What if the tear hadn't worked? I mean, it could have been just a plain old crystal, and we'd all be dead by now."

"No. The pegasus said she would protect us. She promised, and a pegasus doesn't lie."

"But Bombax does," says Petra. "That's who poisoned Brutus and opened the kamadan's cage. And he won't quit till we're dead."

"What are we going to do, Petra?"

1) "We can leave, get away before they kill us, and try to warn the king." Turn to page 112.

2) "Or we can stay and tell Romney what's happening." Turn to page 37.

You look at the evil in Bombax's eyes. It seems that he knows everything. Then, almost without thought, you start running.

Angry cries ring out and hands reach for you. At last, slowed by the weight of your disguise, you stumble and fall.

"Move aside!" demands Bombax, looming over you. "What's going on here?" he hisses as he turns your face toward him. Fear fills you as the makeup smears under his touch.

"A disguise? What treachery is this?" he roars as he cruelly rubs your face.

"So it's you," he says quietly. "I never even guessed. If you hadn't run, you might have escaped. But now it's too late."

Grasping your shoulder tightly, he turns to the crowd that has gathered. "Get back to work, all of you. Crabmen, grab the others."

Your friends are seized.

Bombax hurries the four of you to the fortune-teller's tent and thrusts you through the entrance.

Inside, a woman draped in shawls sits at a table, holding a deck of cards.

"Come in, my dears. I've been expecting you," she says quietly. "Come closer. I'm going to tell your fortunes—for free."

As she shuffles the cards, you wonder numbly if you and your friends have a future, or if it's . . .

THE END

98

"Caspius, listen to me," you say as you stroke the owlbear's coarse fur. "We know now who killed Brutus, and we need your help to catch him. You'd like that, wouldn't you?"

Caspius leaps at the bars of the cage and roars loudly.

"Does it understand, Romney?" Petra asks.

"I'm not sure. Owlbears aren't dumb, but they are ruled by their emotions. If they're hungry, they eat whatever's at hand. If they're hurt, they strike out at whatever's nearest."

"Well, I think Caspius will help us," you say confidently.

"I hope so," sighs Romney. "There won't be a second chance if we fail. Right now, there's naught to be gained by worrying. Let's try to get some rest. We don't have long."

All too soon, night falls and Petra struts before you. "Look, Laela. Isn't my costume wonderful? Hurry, or we'll be late!" Flashing an excited grin at you, he climbs down the ladder and disappears.

Quickly you change into your forest-green costume. Touching its velvety softness calms you, and after running a carved comb through your tangled blond hair, you are ready. You stare into your own blue eyes in the mirror. "I will not be afraid," you whisper determinedly to yourself. "I'll do whatever is necessary."

Your determination carries you through the griffon and cat acts.

"Superb!" whispers Romney. "We shall be victorious."

Then Bombax steps into center ring.

"Ladies and gentlemen, your attention please. Bombax Brothers' is proud to present Laela, Petra, and Caspius, the dancing owl-bear. Because of the danger involved, we ask you for complete silence. Any noise, no matter how small, may distract the creature and arouse its savage instincts.

"And now, appearing for the first time anywhere, LAELA AND PETRA!"

In the sudden hush, the torches cast a golden glow on you and Caspius as you step into the ring. The huge creature dwarfs you as it rears up on its massive hind legs. Tugging on the great iron chain, you lead the animal to the center of the ring and face it.

"Down, Caspius," you whisper, and the owlbear drops to all fours. You take a small key from a pocket and, with a swift motion, remove the heavy, clanking chain from the jeweled collar. The audience gasps.

"What, the—" grunts Bombax.

Suddenly, a thin, sweet piping is heard. It makes you think of clouds reflected in a quiet stream and the smell of flowers on a soft summer day. Another torch is lighted, and it outlines Petra, sitting cross-legged on a pedestal and playing a golden flute. You take Caspius's enormous paw into your own small hand, and you both begin to dance.

Round and round the two of you float to the golden tune. You know that you must make a move soon to carry out your plan. But as the

two of you follow the magical piping, you feel the grief draining out of Caspius, and you hesitate to interrupt the healing.

Lost in your own wonderful, warm world of peace, you're shattered when a terrible, shrill noise cuts through Petra's piping and vibrates inside your head like a thousand whistles gone mad. Darkness descends on your mind, and you sink to your knees, certain that you will either die or go mad.

Then you hear a roar, followed by a coarse yell of fear and a gurgling noise that ends abruptly. You lift your hands from your ears and look about in confusion.

Chaos reigns. As more torches are hastily lit, you see people running in all directions. A few leap into the center ring, waving swords. Crabmen edge forward, carrying ropes and chains. Romney stands stunned, staring in horror as Caspius clutches Bombax in a fearsome embrace.

Swords and chains are slowly lowered, and the would-be rescuers come to a sudden halt. Everyone gazes in disbelief at the large silver whistle that Bombax clutches in his fat fist. Slowly the thick fingers open, and the whistle drops to the dust.

"Enough, Caspius, enough," Romney says quietly, and after a long moment, the huge creature allows Bombax's lifeless body to be drawn from its grasp.

Hours later, you and Petra join Romney at the small table in his wagon.

"I don't understand why Bombax blew that whistle," argues Petra. "He knew that either Caspius would kill us all or we would die of madness. How did he expect to get away with that in front of everyone?"

"Easily," Romney answers. "He hid in the shadows, thinking he'd be undetected. But he forgot that owlbears can see in the dark. He never stood a chance. Owlbears also have very sensitive ears. The whistle caused Caspius pain, so the animal stopped the noise in the only way it knew."

"Our plan wouldn't have worked any better, except for Bombax, of course," says Petra. "The way the governor stepped in and took control was great."

"I was glad he believed us," you say.

"Yeah. And did you see Clusia's face when the guards took him away?" chuckles Petra.

"I was more interested in what the governor had to say about the circus coming under the king's protection if no heirs can be found," says Romney. "That would be good.

"But right now, it's time for certain young circus stars to go to bed."

Smiling happily, you stumble drowsily to your bunk. As your eyes close, you drift into a dream of you and Caspius dancing merrily to the music of the magic flute.

THE END

"So you want to be trapeze artists," says the handsome young man as he strokes his carefully waxed mustache. "Well, you've come to the right place. I, Bebiana, am the best there is. But why do you wish to learn? It is difficult. Perhaps you cannot do it. Certainly you'll never be as good as I am." And flexing his smooth muscles, he admires himself in the full-length mirror that hangs on the wall of his house wagon.

"It's because you are the best that we wish to study under you. We know we'll never be as good as you are," you say, placing a firm hand on Petra as he squirms beside you. "But if we work at it very hard, perhaps we'll be a credit to you. Then everyone will say what a good teacher you are."

"Hmmm. You're right," says Bebiana as he smooths his tunic over his chest. "I'm sure I'd be a perfectly marvelous teacher—I'm superb at everything I do. All right, you may stay. But you must always do exactly as I tell you and keep out of my way when we're not practicing.

"First, take these soiled costumes down to the stream and wash them. Be very careful of the decorations—don't lose any of them. And then you can tidy the wagon. I'm afraid I've been too busy to pay much attention to it lately." Tossing a large bundle of soiled clothes in your direction, he gives his glossy blond hair a final pat, and leaves.

"Laela, how could you let him talk to you

like that!" explodes Petra. "That stuck-up, muscular horsetail!

"'You'll never be as good as I am,'" mimics Petra. "I'm the best. I'm superb. I'm magnificent. I'm a pompous donkey!" he snorts, flinging himself down in disgust on the rumpled bunk.

Hysterical woofing cries and loud clapping follow Petra's words.

"What the—!" exclaims Petra. And together you peer under the bed.

Two mischievous black eyes stare back.

"Why, it's that monkey creature!" you say. "What did the ringmaster call it during the show last night?"

"Catcher," says Petra as he pulls the furry animal toward him.

Wuffling softly, it wraps its long arms around Petra's neck and hugs him tightly.

"Why is it under the bed?" you ask.

"It looks as though that's where Bebiana keeps it," Petra says, picking at the silver chain looped around Catcher's neck.

As the lock clicks open and the chain falls away, Catcher shrieks happily and bounces rapidly around the small wagon.

"Quick, catch it!" hollers Petra, and for the next few minutes, madness reigns.

"Whew! Now we know why Bebiana keeps it chained."

"If you do that again, Catcher, I'll have to lock you up," Petra warns.

Catcher looks down and chatters sadly.

"Then behave yourself, and we won't do it," you say, ruffling Catcher's long red fur.

"Laela, maybe this won't work," Petra says suddenly. "Bebiana will never teach us anything. He even uses a monkey as a partner so that he doesn't have to compete with another person. The only thing he'll let us do is be his personal slaves. I don't want to be a trapeze artist if it means bowing and scraping to that conceited bore."

"I don't think it will be that bad, Petra. I think we can work around him and learn in spite of him. Besides, what choice do we have?"

1) "We can become animal trainers," says Petra. Turn to page 47.

2) "We can work in the sideshow." Turn to page 86.

3) "Or we can stay right here and be trapeze artists," you say. Turn to page 108.

"Get her!" screams Bombax as you run into the darkness. Terror-stricken, you turn a corner. There in front of you is the cook's tent. Seated at a table are Helix and Momo.

Tottering forward on shaky legs, you gasp "Help!" and collapse at Helix's feet.

"Laela!" cries Helix, gathering you up.

"Give me that mummy!" screams Bombax.

"This is my daughter, and she stays here with me. What have you done with my son?"

"Son? Daughter? They're freaks! They're mine! I can do anything I want with them!" snarls Bombax as he tugs at your arm.

Suddenly, a large red pincer appears at either side of Bombax's fat neck.

"AAAWKKK!" squawks Bombax as he tries to pry the claws apart.

"Put him in a cage, Anomura," says Helix. And the crabman marches Bombax away.

"Where's Petra?" Momo asks worriedly.

"He's out there with Clusia and Madame Leone and two dopplegangers!" you cry.

"Who'll help me rescue my son?" yells Helix.

"We will!" shout the workers as they grab tools and knives and crowd to his side.

Placing you in Momo's warm embrace, Helix says, "Stay here, dear. We'll be right back. Don't worry. Everything's going to be OK."

As you sink into Momo's loving arms, you know that you are home at last.

THE END

"Well, let's get started," you say as you roll up your sleeves. "I don't think he's EVER cleaned this place!"

Hours later, you look about happily. The woodwork gleams, fresh linens cover the bed, and a stew bubbles on the stove.

"I hope that pompous parrot appreciates what we've done," Petra says with a sigh. "I guess we'll find out soon—here he comes."

"You, girl. Have you done the wash?"

"Yes, sir, and I've mended it, too. Everything's here in the closet, ready to be worn."

"I hope you were careful. I know how irresponsible children are," Bebiana says.

The aerialist abruptly stops talking as he takes a good look around the sparkling wagon.

"How did you do this?" he demands. "Are you an illusionist's apprentice?"

"No, sir. We did it with soap and water."

"Very clever. What's this?" Lifting the lid off the kettle, he sniffs the stew.

"Yes, well, perhaps I was a bit hasty. Mended it all, too, you say. Hmmm. Maybe I can make something out of you after all. Here. Change into these practice outfits," he orders. "It's time for your first lesson." He tosses some clothes on the bunk, then begins to sample the stew.

"Petra, I feel funny in this," you say once you've donned your outfit.

"You'll get used to it," Petra says soothingly. "There's no way you can be a trapeze artist and wear a long skirt."

"No time for chattering. Follow me, and do everything I do," Bebiana commands as he swaggers out of the wagon.

Petra puffs out his chest, links arms with Catcher, and struts behind Bebiana in a perfect imitation of the pompous performer. Giggling, you trail along behind the small parade toward the main tent.

"Now, this is called rosin," says Bebiana as he shows you how to rub the chalky stuff on your fingers and palms. "It's very important because your life can depend upon it. It'll keep your hands from slipping. Sometimes it's the only thing between you and death. Don't ever forget to use it."

You look at the dry substance and hope you always remember its importance.

"Watch. This is the correct way to climb the ladder." And for the next several hours, you learn how to climb, how to balance, how to sit on the trapeze, and how to swing back and forth with perfect timing.

To your surprise, Bebiana is an excellent teacher, a superb athlete, and probably as good a trapeze artist as he thinks he is.

You discover that if you do not look at the ground—which is only ten feet below the practice bar—you can do most of what you are told. And if you concentrate, it is almost possible to believe that you are just hanging from a rope swing.

Working with Petra is harder, and frequently, when you try to clasp his hands for a basic catch, you miss and fall. But as the afternoon wears on, you begin to learn, and you fall less often.

"I don't think I've ever been so sore in my whole life," groans Petra as he sinks to the ground, long hours later.

"I know what you mean," you say as you massage your aching legs. "But think of how much we've learned. We can already swing from our knees and do simple forward catches. I even did that front forward flip once."

"But you fell. You missed my hands."

"I didn't miss your hands. You forgot to put rosin on them. I caught them, then slipped. I'm just glad we were only a few feet off the ground, or I'd have been hurt."

"Laela, don't nag," moans Petra, covering his ears with his hands.

"There you are, you two. Break's over," Bebiana orders. "Bombax just told me that he wants you in tonight's show. I tried to tell him you weren't ready, but it didn't do any good. So I want you to keep practicing that routine you've been working on."

"But, Bebiana, we've never been higher than ten feet off the ground! How can we possibly do it?" you ask in horror.

"Don't worry, Laela. There's a net. Even if we fall, we'll be all right," Petra says.

"Net? You mean you don't know?" whispers Bebiana, his face turning white and pinched.

"Know what?" you ask as an icy coldness fills your heart.

"There is no net," Bebiana says softly, looking at you with pity.

"Of course there's a net. I've seen it," yells Petra. "It's on the ground at the foot of the center pole."

"That's not a net—it's a lurker above," Bebiana says bitterly. "It's Bombax's idea of added thrills. It stretches out under the trapezes, and the gods help whoever falls."

"What do lurkers do?" you ask fearfully.

"They crush and eat whatever they catch. Sometimes they shake the platform poles. You have to be on guard for that."

"But no net?" you ask with despair.

"No net," says Bebiana, avoiding your eyes, and he turns and walks away.

"Oh, Petra, what do we do now? Performing with a net would be bad enough, but with the lurker waiting for us to fall—I don't know if I can do it!"

"We don't have too many choices, Laela.

1) "We can do it the way Bombax says and take our chances." Turn to page 69.

2) We can try to figure out a way to disarm the lurker." Turn to page 42.

3) "Or we can get out before Bombax kills us." Turn to page 112.

"Petra, don't look up. Just walk into the forest. Pretend you're cheering me up."

Petra does as you ask. Laughing and clowning, he draws you into the nearby woods. Once among the trees, you begin to run.

"Hurry, Petra!" you urge. "There are two pegasi above us. They've come for us."

"I don't see them," Petra says, "but I hope you're right. Bombax is following us."

At last you stumble into a small clearing, and there before you stand the pegasi.

"Now it is my turn to save your lives," says the smaller of the two. "This is my brother, Thunderbolt, and I am known as Quicksilver. Leap upon our backs before it is too late. The enemy approaches."

"Quick!" cries Petra, and he boosts you up onto Quicksilver's back. Then, with a running start, he leaps to the space between Thunderbolt's silvery wings.

"Wrap your hands in our manes and do not look down," directs Quicksilver as she takes a few running steps, then lightly, seemingly without effort, unfolds her shimmering wings and rises into the air. Gaining height rapidly, the pegasi circle the clearing as Bombax and Clusia burst out of the forest.

Wrapping your arms tightly about Quicksilver's neck, you look down from the dizzying height and watch as your enemies disappear from sight.

Leaning forward, you whisper, "Thank you for coming back."

"A promise is a promise," answers the pegasus. "Now, where do you wish to go?"

"To the king. Can you take us there?"

"I can take you anywhere," answers Quicksilver. "But why do you choose man? Man is dangerous. Man kills and destroys."

"You could live with us in our nest," says Thunderbolt. "There are no people there."

"I'm afraid we can't," you say gently. "We must see the king and prevent Bombax from harming others as he did Quicksilver."

"To the king, then," says Thunderbolt as he and his sister soar into the sky.

Astride the powerful pegasus, you ride the wild winds, filled with both excitement and terror as the earth unfolds beneath you.

All too soon the towers of the king's castle appear. After circling the white marble building, the pegasi descend smoothly and land in a small courtyard.

Bowing before you, Quicksilver whispers, "My debt is paid, earth child, but should you need me again, you have but to call. Farewell." And Quicksilver and Thunderbolt prance into the sky and are gone.

"Most visitors come in the door," says a voice. "But then, few come by pegasus."

Turning, you see an old man dressed in ermine. On his head is a jeweled crown.

"Your majesty," you both say, bowing low.

"We've come to warn you of a plot against the kingdom. There are plans to replace you as king," Petra blurts out.

"That's not a bad idea," sighs the king, taking off the heavy crown and placing it on a bench. "There are always plots to take over the kingdom. If those fools knew what a burden it is, they'd pay me to keep the job."

Rubbing his forehead wearily, he sinks down on the bench. "Tell me about this plot. I suppose I'll have to stop it."

"It's the circus that's coming tomorrow. And dopplegangers! We heard everything!" cries Petra. And the tale is soon told.

"The circus, eh? That's too bad. I was looking forward to it. I enjoyed the circus when I was a prince—cinnamon apples, clowns, mastodons. Ahh, I wish I were still a prince. I've half a mind to give the fools what they seek and go off on my own. Be a plain person, or maybe be a clown," muses the king.

"Your majesty, you wouldn't really do that, would you?" you ask nervously.

"No, unfortunately, I wouldn't," the king says with a sigh. "But even kings can dream.

"Come along, you two. Thanks to you, the kingdom is saved. And once this is all over, there will be two places here at the castle for a girl and boy. It's not as interesting as the circus, but I hope you'll stay. Think about it."

There doesn't seem to be much to think about. A home at the castle sounds fine to you!

THE END

Clutching the tear in your hand, you whisper,
"Pegasus, please help us."

Before the words fade, there is a rush of
wind, and two pegasi stand before you.

"We are at your command," says the smaller
of the two.

"We need your help to rescue Bebiana and
Catcher," you cry as you rush to its side.

"Climb upon our backs and do not fear,"
says the pegasus.

You grip the silvery mane and clamber up
on the broad back. The creature springs
upward, and the ground falls away. Far below,
you see Bombax run into the center of the
arena and point at you. You feel a tingling jolt,
then nothing. When you look down again, you
see Bombax surrounded by crabmen, who
hold him firmly in their pincers.

Then you are hovering next to the trembling
Catcher and the terrified aerialist.

Petra edges his mount closer until Bebiana
is able to slip onto the pegasus. Wrapping his
arms around Petra's waist, he shudders with
relief and says, "All right, I'm safe. Let's go."

"No, we're not done yet," you answer.

"Leave the ape. It tried to kill me!"

"Catcher," you call quietly. Catcher turns
away and tries to climb higher. But there is
nowhere left to go.

"Catcher, I know Bombax put a spell on you
and made you do it. I'll explain. It'll be all
right. Please come down. Please."

Slowly, the great head turns. Tear-filled

eyes peer at you, and Catcher twitters sadly.

"I know you didn't mean to do it, Catcher. Please trust me. Please come down."

Slowly the long fingers loosen their hold, and the great creature steps onto the pegasus. The pegasus shudders as the animal settles its great weight behind you.

"Pegasus, dear friend, please take us to the king," you say, and the pegasus lands gracefully before the royal box.

"Never have I seen such bravery," says the king. "You shall have the ten gold pieces and more." Then a frown crosses his face. "Unless this is part of the show."

"Yes! It's part of the show!" screams Bombax as he struggles to free himself.

"No! It's not part of the show," you say firmly as everyone talks at once.

"QUIET!" commands the king, and silence falls. "Now, one at a time, each of you may speak, and no one may interrupt."

Soon the tale is told, and although Bombax speaks convincingly, the evidence is all against him. Even Clusia, seeking to save himself, turns against the circus owner. "Bombax made me do it. I'm innocent!"

"Take them away!" the king sharply orders his guards.

Turning, he says, "Crabmen, you are free to return to your village with my blessing and my vow of protection. Go in peace.

"Pegasi, noble creatures, from this day forth, you and your kind will be protected in all the forests of Greyhawk. No man may trap or trade you. Be free.

"Laela, Petra. Your courage has saved the kingdom. The evil dopplegangers shall be routed out. Bombax and Clusia shall be placed where they cannot harm anyone, and all will be well with the kingdom. But what can I do for you? How may I reward you?"

"Your majesty, sir," mumbles Petra. "What's going to happen to the circus? Is there some way we could stay with it?"

"A fine idea," says the king. "I like circuses myself. We'll make this the official circus of Greyhawk. But we can't have you wandering about the country without supervision.

"Bebiana, I place you in charge of these children. I hold you personally responsible for their training and their well-being. Considering the way they rescued you today, I'm sure you consider it a small price to pay. Am I correct?"

"Oh, yes, sir! Wonderful children. It's the least I can do," says Bebiana, gritting his teeth.

"But don't forget," he whispers to you. "I still get top billing."

Holding Catcher's furry hands in your own, you and Petra bow to the king and smile happily at your great good luck.

THE END

Throughout the long night, the two of you argue whether to go or to stay. As morning dawns, Petra sighs. "I agree we should help Helix, Momo, and the king, but I don't really care what happens to anyone else. No one's cared about us. Why do we have to care?"

"Because people SHOULD care about each other. We can't turn our backs on the world. Besides, Momo and Helix like us."

"All right. I give up!" cries Petra. "But if it were up to me alone, I'd stay here."

Sometime before dawn breaks, you tell Silverhawk of your decision.

"I am sorrowed," he says gently. "But perhaps it's for the best." Raising his great head, he says, "Come. If we are to help you, now is the time."

Excitement tingles in your veins as you climb onto your pegasus's back. Swiftly the herd of pegasi soars into the morning sky, filling it with white wings and silver manes.

The herd descends sharply through a thick bank of clouds. As the clouds break, you see the king's castle and, camped near it, the circus.

Without pause, the pegasi plunge earthward, pulling up just short of death.

Looking about dazedly, you realize that you have landed next to Bombax's wagon. You watch in amazement as four muscular stallions surround the wagon and rapidly reduce it to nothing more than kindling with powerful blows from their sharp hooves.

Crouched near the ruins, Bombax cowers in fear as Silverhawk's hooves thunder down within inches of his face. Then one of the young stallions grasps Bombax's nightshirt and rises into the air.

A wail of terror issues from Bombax as his fat figure dangles against the cold morning sky. Sleepy circus folk pour from their wagons as the pegasi fill the sky.

Like a silver streak, the pegasi circle the towers of the castle, then rise higher and higher into the sky.

Your pegasus flies alongside Bombax, and you hear Silverhawk say, "You are an evil man. You have brought pain, suffering, and death to man and animal alike. For this, you will die. One who values the precious gift of life so little should not enjoy it himself."

"No! NO! WAIT!" screams Bombax. "Please! I promise I'll be better!"

"Silverhawk! Don't drop him!" you cry.

"Why should you plead for his worthless life?" asks Silverhawk.

"Because killing him would lessen you," answers Petra. "Give Bombax to the king and let him him decide the punishment. You wouldn't like it if men decided the fate of a pegasus."

"You are wise for being the child of man," replies Silverhawk.

Then the herd circles once more, descends in a wide, smooth sweep, and lands in the innermost courtyard of the castle.

Before long, you are surrounded by hundreds of sleepy members of the court, including a yawning king.

"Please, please don't let them get me," blubbers Bombax as he crawls to the king and flings himself at his feet. "Protect me, your majesty. I'll tell you anything you want to know."

"This should be interesting," the king says dryly.

Tears well up in your throat as you bid farewell to your pegasus. Throwing your arms around her neck, you rest your face on her muzzle. "Oh, pegasus, will I ever see you again?"

"You never lose that which you love," the creature answers. "As long as I am in your thoughts, I am with you."

Through a blur of tears, you see the pegasi rise into the sky, and then they are gone.

"Well, young lady, young sir. I generally depend on more normal ways of waking, but if the story behind all this is half as interesting as the method of delivery, I promise not to interrupt once. Now," he says, placing his arms around your shoulders, "can I interest you in breakfast?

"Guards, take this man away!"

THE END

Opening your mouth, you grunt and whimper piteously while pawing at the front of Bombax's tunic.

"Don't touch me!" Bombax shrieks, leaping backward and frantically brushing at his chest with a silk handkerchief. "You freak! It could be catching! I don't want to be a mummy!" Throwing the handkerchief on the ground, he fixes you with a look of horror and rushes away.

You're more than pleased with Bombax's reaction, but fortunately, the stiff goop on your face prevents you from smiling.

Coughing, or perhaps laughing behind his hand, Helix takes you by the arm and guides you away from the fortune-teller's tent.

"Very good! You've passed the first test. I was worried there for a minute, but I don't know why—even your own mothers wouldn't recognize you," murmurs Helix.

"If we HAD mothers," mumbles Petra.

Please turn to page 74.

"Maybe the crabman will help us," you say to Petra, pulling him toward Anomura.

"We'll catch him in the act!" the crabman exclaims excitedly after you explain the situation to him. "I'll gather my men. You stay here. It's safer."

"We'll miss all the action if we stay here, and that's not fair," argues Petra. "You wouldn't even know about this if it weren't for us. We're going, too!"

"All right," sighs Anomura, "but at least stay on the pegasi. I don't want you underfoot if there's violence."

Riding the pegasus, you follow the crowd of crabmen out of the big top and into the brightly lit sideshow. As you turn a corner, you see Bombax ushering the king into a tent.

"You guards stay outside for a while," Bombax says. "It's quite safe. The king is going to have his fortune told." The guards shrug and stand on either side of the door.

As the crabmen spread out, you see two corn vendors sneaking forward.

"Anomura," you whisper, and as the crabman turns, you point out the vendors.

Quickly, before they even know anyone is aware of their evil presence, the vendors are seized in the crabmen's great pincers and dragged away, struggling helplessly.

Seconds later, Bombax sticks his head out of the tent and looks about worriedly.

"Looking for someone?" asks Anomura.

"No one you'd know," Bombax snarls.

"You'd be surprised," says Anomura as he gestures toward the captured corn vendors.

"Release those men!" Bombax sputters.

"We told them the whole story," Petra says from his pegasus. "Let the king go."

"Never!" shrieks Bombax. "No snot-nosed children are going to ruin my great plan." And dropping the tent flap, he disappears.

"After him!" yells Anomura, and the tent is rushed by guards and crabmen alike. It totters crazily and then collapses, billowing in all directions as fighting breaks out beneath its striped folds. A moment later, Bombax slithers out from under the far edge, dragging the king behind him.

Within seconds, a pegasus stands on either side of Bombax. No matter which way he turns, their sharp hooves block his path. At last, Petra's pegasus pins Bombax to the ground and says, "Cease." Bombax gives up and releases his hold on the king.

The king sits up and rubs his throat. "I can only guess what has gone on here," he says. "But it is obvious to me that you have saved my life. You have but to make a wish, and it will be granted."

As the guards and the crabmen fight their way free of the tent, you and Petra and the king smile at each other. And all at once you know, deep in your heart, that everything will be all right.

THE END

The next morning, Rebus Romney wakens
you while he prepares coffee and hot porridge.
"I think we should begin your training today,"
he says. "There's no good reason to wait."

"What are we going to learn, sir?" you ask
as you hop out of your narrow bunk.

"Something simple. Probably owlbears."

"Simple?" asks a tousled Petra. "I thought
owlbears were killers."

"If you give them the chance. But they're
really quite stupid. And they're greedy. Gems
and food are their weaknesses. We keep them
well fed and give them a pouch of phony jewels after each performance. That keeps them
happy. So if you avoid their claws and jaws,
you're fairly safe.

"Eat up now, and let's get started!"

The two of you do as you are bid, and soon
the breakfast dishes stand neatly stacked in
the gaily painted cupboards.

As you walk toward the animal cages,
Romney says, "Just watch me. I'll run through
the act once so you can see how it's done."

Stopping before the owlbears' red cage,
Romney stands to the side of the door and
swings it open. In one hand, he holds a large
chunk of overripe meat; in the other, a heavy
chain.

Holding the meat with his fingertips, the
trainer dangles it in front of the open door,
then deftly lets go as five razor-sharp claws
whistle through the air.

Falling upon the meat, the owlbear never

even notices as Romney slips up and hooks the chain to its gem-studded collar.

"Here," Romney says, handing the chain to Petra. "Its name is Brutus. When it's through eating, take it into the center ring. Laela, we'll get you its brother, Caspius."

"Take this," says Romney, handing you a chunk of meat. "You try it. You saw how I did it. Mind you, watch out for its claws."

"Here, boy. Here, Caspius," you call hesitantly as you waggle the reeking meat in front of the open cage door.

With a great roar, Caspius leaps upon the meat, ripping it from your trembling fingers.

"Quick, girl. Snap that chain on while it's busy with the meat," urges Romney. And, though frightened, you do as you are told.

"Now grab the end of the chain and head toward the tent. Good Caspius. Bring your treat with you. That's a good owlbear."

In the center ring, the animals tower over you and Petra, their red-rimmed eyes burning brightly. Swaying from side to side, Brutus lowers its head and growls at Petra.

"No! Never give them a chance to do that!" shouts Romney, leaping into the ring and grabbing the chain from Petra. "Here, let me take it for a minute. Laela, follow me. Do exactly as I do!"

Moving ahead of the shambling owlbear, Romney leads the fearful creature around the ring in a series of dancelike movements.

Following a few steps behind, you do your

best to imitate the trainer's moves. For a time, both owlbears perform gracefully and obediently. Then, without warning, Romney's bear gives an agonized roar, clutches its stomach with both paws, and collapses.

"What, the—!" exclaims the trainer, dashing to the fallen beast.

Shrieking with pain and rage, the animal clubs the trainer with its huge paws, sweeping him toward its massive body. Crying piteously, the creature clutches the trainer in a deadly embrace.

"Help me! Do something!" gasps Romney as the bear draws him toward its gaping beak.

1) "Don't move, Laela. I'll tangle it up in this," cries Petra as he spies a large gray net. Turn to page 58.

2) "Run, Laela!" Petra orders. "There's nothing we can do." Turn to page 31.

3) "I'll use the tear!" you cry. Turn to page 95.

Later in the morning, Bebiana has a surprise announcement for you. "I think it's a mistake," he snarls, "but Bombax wants you to take part in the command performance before the king this evening."

"Probably because we'll be so bad that we'll make you look even better," Petra says.

"That must be it," Bebiana says. "What other reason could there be? You two practice. I'm going to decide which costume I should wear tonight," he says as he hurries away. "The blue matches my eyes, but the red sets off my hair . . . but then. . . ."

"I don't know what Bombax is planning," you tell Petra, "but this is the chance we've been looking for. If the king is here tonight, we just have talk to him and tell him what's going on."

For the rest of the day, you practice all that Bebiana has taught you. By nightfall, you are much improved.

In the flickering torchlight, you scan the tent, trying to locate the king.

"There he is! Look!" Petra whispers excitedly. You follow his pointing finger and see a small, tired-looking man wearing a gold crown. He's surrounded by guards.

"Out of my way, urchins!" snarls Bebiana as he and Catcher swarm up the pole. "Watch the master. Maybe you'll learn something."

Petra kicks the pole in anger, but as much as you hate to admit it, Bebiana IS superb. You're as enthralled as the audience by his flights through the air with the very greatest of ease.

Then, just before Bebiana's finale, something goes wrong. Catcher—mild, gentle, dependable Catcher—sits up abruptly, as though shocked.

You hear Bebiana curse Catcher and demand that the animal return to its position.

"Petra, what's wrong? Catcher never does anything like that."

"Laela, look!" replies Petra.

In the shadows, not twenty paces away, stands Bombax. You notice with alarm that his attention is concentrated on Catcher.

"Petra," you whisper nervously, "something bad's going to happen. We've got to stop it."

"How? Nothing's happened yet. Maybe we're imagining it. If we interrupt Bebiana's act, he'll kill us. Then we won't have to worry about Bombax."

"But if we don't act and he's hurt or killed, I'll never forgive myself."

1) "I say do nothing," says Petra. "He's not very nice to us. Let him take care of himself." Turn to page 26.

2) "I can't just stand here and watch. I'm going to try to warn him." Turn to page 155.

"Do we have to go by ourselves?" you ask nervously.

"No, of course not. What are families for?" answers Helix with a smile.

Minutes later, the three of you crouch behind a wagon filled with hay. You have a perfect view of the fortune-teller's tent. You have to wait only a few moments before Petra whispers excitedly, "Two corn vendors are coming."

Wordlessly, the three of you watch as the silent figures look both ways, then enter the tent. "And here come Bombax, Clusia, and two other men," you whisper.

With a great flourish, Bombax ushers the two men into the fortune-teller's tent.

As you watch the silent tent, the skin on the back of your neck prickles, and you feel cold. The very air seems to crackle with danger. Then the feeling vanishes. Seconds later, Bombax leaves Madame Leone's tent. His broad face is wreathed in smiles, and the two men who walk beside him seem slightly different in some indefinable manner.

A few minutes later, Clusia leaves the tent, carrying two corn vendors' boxes. Looking about sneakily, he tries to hide the boxes under his cloak, then hurries away.

"I've seen all that I need to," says Helix grimly. "Unless I'm mistaken, we just saw two harmless people taken over by dopplegangers. I think it's time for a full meeting of circus regulars. We have to do something before this goes any further."

"But, Helix, will the circus people come? Will they believe you?" you ask.

"They might be difficult to convince," admits Helix. "It's a pretty strange story. But circus folks stick together in times of trouble, and no one likes Bombax.

"Now you two go back and stay with Mother. She'll be worried about you."

"But, Helix," you protest, "that's not fair. We want to see what happens."

"You may have a point there," says Helix, "but I have a point, too."

"What's that?" Petra asks defiantly.

"No children of mine are going to be in dangerous situations if I have anything to say about it."

"Ch-children . . . of yours?" you and Petra stutter together.

"That's what I said, and that's what I mean. If it's all right with you," Helix says as you and Petra fling your arms about his thin body and hug him tightly.

"Is this any way to treat your poor old father?" gasps Helix.

You just smile. For the first time in your life, you know that everything will turn out all right.

THE END

"Laela, we're not good enough yet. And they're each too heavy for you to hold."

"We must try, Petra. I'm strong enough."

Quickly you climb the pole and seat yourself on the waiting trapeze. Directly across from you, Petra does the same. You flex your knees and pump your trapeze higher and higher. Above you, Catcher and Bebiana struggle to cling to the thin rope.

You keep pumping until your outstretched toes brush the canvas an inch from Bebiana's face. As you reach the highest possible point, you let go of the trapeze ropes and drop backward. Clinging tightly to the trapeze bar with the back of your knees, you hang upside down above the arena. Blood rushes to your head as you hold out your hands and cry, "Grab my hands!"

Catcher gibbers in fear, and Bebiana seems unable to move.

"Bebiana, grab my hands! There's still a chance people will think this is an act!"

Appealing to Bebiana's vanity works! Cautiously, he crawls down Catcher's back and times your approach. At the height of your swing, Bebiana drops. As he falls, your hands lock about each other's wrists. The full weight of his body jerks against you. For a moment you fear you will drop him, but then he releases you, does a single somersault, and is expertly caught by Petra. Out of the corner of your eye you see Bebiana land on the platform and take a deep bow.

Again you swing back and forth until you are close enough to touch Catcher.

"Catcher! Come on! Don't be scared! We got Bebiana down, and we can get you down, too." But Catcher just whimpers.

"Laela, the only thing it knows how to do is catch," Petra calls from his trapeze.

"Then what are we to do?"

"Let it catch you, and we'll take it from there," calls Petra. Reluctantly, you agree.

As Petra tells Catcher the plan, you try to still your wildly beating heart. If the plan works—if Catcher understands—all will be well. But if it fails, you'll both fall.

Dangerous or not, you'll do your best to make the plan succeed, or die trying.

"I'm coming, Catcher," you cry as you push yourself off in one last swing. At your highest point, you extend your arms, say a quick prayer, and let go of the trapeze bar.

Like a slingshot rock, you shoot through the air. Just as you begin to lose momentum, your ankles are gripped by two bands of steel. At the very same instant, Petra flies to meet you, and your hands clasp each other's wrists. Then, as Catcher lets go of the rope and hangs from your ankles, it feels as if you are being torn in half.

Slower and slower you swing, with the great weight finally bringing the trapeze to a halt. The three of you cling to one another, unable to move forward or back.

"We're doomed!" cries Petra.

"Pegasus, help us!" you whisper.

Incredibly, Catcher's weight is suddenly removed from your ankles. As you gasp in relief, the silvery form of the pegasus is at your side. "Climb on my back behind the ape, little one," the rescuer whispers.

Miraculously, a second pegasus appears beneath Petra. Then the pegasi circle the tent and land in front of the king.

"Excellent! Superb!" cries the king. "You had me completely convinced. I thought you were in danger. By gad! What an act!"

"B-B-But, your majesty!" you stammer. "It wasn't an act. We WERE in danger!"

"Nonsense! Of course it was an act," insists Bombax as he sweeps you behind him. "Bombax Brothers' Circus always tries to provide the best in entertainment, making what is real and what is not real difficult to discern and always leaving you wondering.

"Now may I suggest that we tour the sideshow? It would give me great pleasure to show you some of its more unusual aspects. You could even have your fortune told. I promise it will be a unique experience."

1) If you want to try to get the king's attention and tell him what is really happening, turn to page 22.

2) If you want to try to rescue the king yourself, turn to page 124.

"Hurry, Laela. I want to be a long way from here by the time Romney gets back," Petra tells you as you leave the wagon.

"I think this is wrong," you say, "but if you really mean to go, I'll go, too."

"We'll follow this trail straight into the forest. No one will find us there," says Petra.

"What's that hanging up there, Petra?" you ask, pointing at a gray mass suspended between two trees above the trail.

"Don't be such a scaredy-cat. It's just an old net someone's drying out," says Petra.

Then, even as you watch, the gray mass detaches itself and flutters downward, trapping you and Petra in its folds. You fight wildly but to no avail. The net heaves for a moment more, then all is still.

"Excellent, Clusia. My compliments on a job well done," says Bombax, stepping from behind a large tree.

"Once more the lurker above does away with a sticky problem and leaves no evidence behind. Too bad the kamadan didn't work, but all's well that ends badly for someone else, as I always say."

THE END

Touching the tear embedded in the mummy skin, you say, "Pegasus, please come."

Seconds later, the tent top splits, and the pegasus lands before you. The creature paws the ground and snorts nervously.

"Don't be afraid. It's me. Look, it's really me," you say, tearing at the mummy skin. As the makeup peels away from your face, the pegasus whickers happily.

"Oh, pegasus, I'm so glad to see you," you cry, tears trembling on your lashes. "You've got to help us. Bombax is going to have the dopplegangers take us over."

"It will be hard to do if he cannot find you. Climb on my back," says the pegasus.

Using a chair, both of you climb onto the animal's back. Then the pegasus leaps out of the tent and into the night sky.

Soon, high atop a mountain peak, you meet Silverhawk, leader of the Greyhawk pegasi.

"We pegasi shun man," says Silverhawk, "because he carries evil and greed in his heart. But you have rescued one who is dear to us. Because of this, I offer you the chance to become one with us."

"What do you mean?" you ask hesitantly.

1) "You can live with us, far from hurtful man." Turn to page 79.

2) "Or if you decide that you cannot leave the world of man, we will grant you one last wish." Turn to page 119.

"Why should we sleep in the woods?" protests Petra. "It's damp and creepy there."

"Would you rather be damp or dead?" you ask, gathering up your long skirt.

"Not much choice when you put it that way," Petra grumbles. "But do you really think Bombax will try something tonight?"

"Do you want to take the chance?"

"No," admits Petra grudgingly as he follows you into the woods.

Finding a clear place in the underbrush, you and Petra lie down and cover yourselves with leaves. Quickly, you both fall asleep.

You're so well hidden by your blanket of leaves that you aren't noticed when four shadowy figures emerge from the woods and watch Bebiana's wagon.

"No sign of them," says Bombax in disgust. "I thought we'd find them here for sure. I admit they're smarter than I thought. But it doesn't matter—they'll be dead by tomorrow, one way or another."

When you wake in the early morning hours, the wagons are ready to roll.

"Hop on, you two, unless you want to be left behind," shouts Bebiana grumpily.

As you swing up beside him onto the wagon seat, you think you vaguely remember hearing Bombax say something threatening about today, but you decide sleepily that you must have been dreaming.

Please turn to page 131.

Bombax stares at you expectantly. "Well, speak up. Don't just stand there like a lump." Gingerly he pokes your shoulder. "What's your name?" he demands. Then his body jerks as he is pushed from behind, and he staggers several steps before falling to the ground.

Petra stands over the prone circus owner in a threatening manner.

"Now, mate, there's no need for that," Helix says soothingly as he draws Petra aside. "Bombax meant no harm. Think before you act. It's safer."

Bending over, he helps Bombax to his feet. "Take no offense, sir. These two are very close, and Clem, here, thought you were trying to hurt his brother."

"Cursed freak!" splutters Bombax, brushing the dirt off his clothes. "Brothers, eh? How can you tell?" Walking over to Petra, he jabs a fat finger at his face. "Listen, you freak. Never touch me again. If you do, you and your ugly brother are both out! Understand?"

You wait tensely until Petra nods yes. Then Bombax turns and strides away.

"You don't know how close you came to harm, lad. I've seen him kill crabmen just for bumping into him. You'll have to control that temper. Bombax is no one to trifle with."

Please turn to page 74.

You hope against hope that Madame Leone won't tell Bombax where you are. But even if she does, you try to convince yourself, Bombax won't really hurt you.

Finally, tired from the effort of arguing with yourself, you curl up in a corner and try to stop thinking.

The stuffy warmth of the enclosed wagon, combined with the darkness, lulls you into a false sense of security. Without meaning to, you fall asleep.

Hours later, you are startled into wakefulness by the sound of someone entering the wagon.

"So," snarls a familiar voice, "you couldn't leave well enough alone. You had to meddle. Well, I told you what happens to meddlers. Now you have no one to blame but yourselves. After all, I can't let you ruin my plans."

Before you can start to struggle, strong arms pull you and Petra from the wagon. You open your mouth to scream, but a hand is clapped over it. As you're led into the dark night, you hear Bombax say, "Well, I think that's the last problem that stands between us and success. Tomorrow should see us victorious, the rulers of Greyhawk."

You've made a bad decision. But maybe you can still do something. Maybe there's still hope, and then again . . . maybe there's not.

THE END

"Don't move. Stand still," you whisper.

The kamadan stops for a moment and screams.

You stand motionless.

Belly to the ground, the kamadan slinks forward, wailing a song of hatred. Sniffing first at you, then at Petra, it snarls, lifting its lips to show long, curved fangs.

Softly, like the murmur of the wind, you begin to croon a melody that you have often used to calm wild and injured creatures.

The cat shrinks back, its ears flattened against its head. Hissing and snarling, it crouches, suddenly undecided. Then the snakes on its shoulders begin to move as one, following you as you sway with the melody.

"Sing, Petra," you whisper urgently.

With Petra's voice joining yours, the soft, soothing melody continues.

The giant cat shakes its head, growls uncertainly, then slowly lies down. Gradually, the rage fades from its eyes and it begins to purr.

Ever so carefully, you edge closer to the ferocious beast, crooning words of comfort. Sinking to your knees in front of the giant cat, you look into its golden eyes and say, "Good boy," as you stretch out your hand.

Extending its head, the kamadan sniffs your hand, then licks it with its rough tongue. Great rumbling purrs echo in its chest as you gently scratch its throat.

"Come on, boy. Time to go back," you say calmly, rising and walking to its cage.

Once you've securely locked the door, you slip your hand between the bars, pet the big cat, and say, "Good boy. I'm proud of you. I'll be back to see you soon."

Turning, you stop in surprise. Marshaled around the cage are performers, crabmen, and sideshow people, each clutching a weapon. Cheering loudly, they surround you.

"We thought you'd be dead!" exclaims a crabman. "That cat's a killer! How did you do it?"

Stunned by the outcry and the press of people, you stutter, "It—it was nothing, really. I treated it as I do any cat."

"I knew you had the gift," says Romney, pushing his way through the crowd. "But I didn't expect you to prove it so soon."

Facing the crowd, he holds up his hands and says, "Thanks for your help, friends. Show time in five minutes."

Then he turns to you and Petra. "I suggest you two go back to my wagon. And try to stay out of mischief until I return."

"But, sir!"

"No 'buts' about it, lad. Do as I say. Cages don't just unlock themselves. I can't do the show if I'm worried about you. Get back to the wagon, lock yourselves in, and stay there until I get back."

Please turn to page 127.

As your hands continue to slip, you realize that you forgot to put rosin on them before you climbed the ladder. You have no one to blame for this but yourself.

You can feel Petra slipping from the bar. Shutting your mind to fear, you open your fingers and slide completely from his grasp.

As you fall toward the waiting lurker, you curl your body into a ball, hoping that you'll be able to escape the monster and that this will not really be . . .

THE END

No one even notices the two of you as you slip out of the tent and run quickly into the forest.

Later—many years later—you look out of the sheltering forest that is your home. You see King Bombax, dressed in jewels and furs, ride by, surrounded by Clusia and his other ministers of state.

"You know, Petra," you say softly as you chew on a root, "I've always wished that we had stayed. Maybe things would have been different. Maybe Bombax and Clusia and all those dopplegangers wouldn't have been able to take over so easily. Now people are all but slaves, and even the land is being destroyed as Bombax plunders it for minerals and gems. Maybe we could have told the king and saved the country."

"Maybe," says Petra as he gnaws on some bark, "but we'll never know."

THE END

For the rest of the day, Romney teaches you and Petra how to work with griffons and their cousins, the hypogriffs.

As the afternoon fades, Romney expresses satisfaction, and after sending the beasts back to the meadow, he draws you to his side.

"You've far exceeded my expectations," he says with a smile. "And if we succeed, you've both got great circus careers ahead of you. Go rest up now. Be back by six bells, don't be late, and stay out of trouble."

Finally six bells chime, and you join Romney in center ring. You are dressed in forest-green tights and a velvet jerkin. Petra is dressed in scarlet and gold.

Townsfolk trickle in, filling the tent to capacity.

"Those two men dressed in purple, sitting in the center box, are the mayor and the governor. We have to get to them," says Romney.

"Ladies and gentlemen and children of all ages," booms Clusia.

"Petra, I'm scared."

"I'm scared, too, Laela, but I'm more afraid of Bombax. We have to do it."

A trumpet blares, and Clusia says, "Ladies and gentlemen, we direct your attention to the center ring, where Petra and Laela, the world's youngest animal trainers, will demonstrate their spectacular abilities with the largest pack of griffons and hypogriffs in captivity! Silence, please!"

Obeying Petra's hidden hand signals, the

king of the griffons lowers its fierce, feathered head so you can hook a hand around the tawny neck. Then you are borne high above the sawdust ring as the immense bird-animal wheels and dips through the air.

You glance down, and the ground seems very far away. The lights blur, and suddenly you are very dizzy. Then, just as your hand starts to slip, the griffon turns and stares at you. Although it does not speak, something passes between the two of you. Some of the creature's fierce independence seems to flow into you, and your fears fall away. Swiftly you climb to the top of the griffon's head and, closing your mind to all but the calm place within you, carefully slide down and drape your body in its open beak.

A gasp goes up from the audience as the savage creature holds you gently in its sharp, hooked beak.

Then, to thunderous applause, you are deposited gently at Petra's feet, and you take your bows with pride and happiness.

"And now, ladies and gentlemen, we ask for two brave volunteers from the audience to join the beautiful Laela on a ride above the three rings of Bombax Brothers' Circus," says Romney. "Speak up. Surely you are not afraid to do what one small girl has done."

The audience stirs nervously. Not one hand can be seen waving above the crowd.

"You gentlemen in purple, surely we can convince you to join us," Romney says, pointing to the surprised mayor and the governor.

Both men look around, hoping that someone else has been singled out.

Clapping and whistling, the audience urges the officials into the ring.

"What's he up to, Clusia?" hisses Bombax from behind you.

"I don't know. Maybe it's just part of a new act. Surely it doesn't mean anything."

"It had better not. Call out the doppelgangers, just in case."

"Now, gentlemen, if you'll kindly step up on this drum and then onto the backs of the griffons. No, I insist. Please climb up," says Romney.

Unwilling to appear cowardly before the audience, the officials hitch their robes above their chubby legs and climb onto the griffons.

"Thank you, gentlemen. And now my young associates and I will join you and perform an act that has never been seen before."

Quickly, before the frightened officials can change their minds, you and Petra climb on behind them. Romney leaps astride a hypogriff, and in an instant, all the powerful creatures soar into the air.

During the next few moments, your flying mounts circle the tent poles at high speed, do aerial somersaults, plummet to within inches of the ground before pulling up, and weave intricate patterns in the air. Then, giving a triumphant screech, Romney's hypogriff strains upward and rips through the canvas

tent top. Within seconds, each of the other airborne beasts follows, leaving behind a silent, dumbstruck audience.

Swiftly the bird-animals cleave the night air, parting pearly clouds like a knife through water. Then, with no warning, the creatures plunge toward the unseen earth.

The mayor shrieks with fear and buries his face deep in the griffon's feathers.

Although you know you should be afraid, you're not. The dark air sings a strange and exciting melody in your ears, and blood pounds in your veins.

All too soon, the proud beasts extend their enormous wings and float to a halt on a high hill, far from the lights of the circus.

"I'll see that you're dead before you get out of prison!" exclaims the mayor as he stumbles off the griffon's back.

"Is there a good reason for this?" asks the governor. "Are we being kidnapped?"

"Only temporarily, sir. If you wish to return to the circus after we tell you our story, we'll take you there," Rebus Romney says politely.

Crouching on the hilltop, the three of you tell your story to the two officials.

"A pack of lies," snarls the mayor. "Who could possibly duplicate me?"

"Just about any donkey in the country," replies the governor. Then he turns to you.

"I believe you. It's a good plan, and had it not been for your courage, it would have worked. Now, if your noble steeds will bear us

154

again, let us fly to the capital with all possible
speed and warn the king. Once he's alerted,
the army can be called out and all of the dopplegangers can be rounded up. It won't be
easy, but it can be done. I shall take part personally in seizing Bombax and Clusia."

"Not I! You'll not catch me getting on one of
those buzzards again," the mayor sputters. "I
can't believe you're going to swallow this ri-
diculous story. You'll be a laughingstock
tomorrow. It's probably just a joke thought up
by these people. Everyone knows that circus
people are scum!"

"Do what you must, Mayor Boffle. I'm
going," says the governor. "I hope you enjoy
the walk home."

Without another word, the four of you climb
onto your waiting mounts and, turning your
faces into the clean north wind, set course for
the capital and the king.

THE END

Ignoring Petra, you climb to the top of the pole. "Bebiana," you call, "come back. Something terrible is going to happen."

"Go away, or I'll do something terrible to you," hisses Bebiana.

"But, Bebiana, something bad is going to happen. Bombax is putting a spell on Catcher. Petra and I saw him do it. Come down."

"When I do come down, I'll deal with you, Petra, AND that crazy monkey. You're all jealous. Go away!" he yells furiously.

Defeated, you climb down the ladder.

"Well, what did he say?" asks Petra.

"He won't listen. He's angry," you reply.

"I told you it wouldn't do any good," snorts Petra. "Well, at least you tried. Now he deserves whatever he gets."

Somehow, you don't find that thought comforting as you look up at the tiny figures so high above the ground, with nothing below to catch them if anything goes wrong.

Please turn to page 26.

You hear soft wufflings and the rustle of hay. Mammoths! Quickly, you seize a branch from a camp fire and run toward the beasts.

As you watch them swaying gently in their sleep, you think about their insane fear of fire. Gathering your courage, you run near them, yelling and waving your torch.

Terrified squeals fill the night air as the huge animals try to escape. Ignoring their fright, you hold the torch to a hairy haunch. There is a stink of burning fur, then a terrible screech of pain. The hurt mammoth rips up its chain and stake, and stampedes. You thrust the torch at one mammoth after another until the last of them disappears.

The wagons are gone, pounded to pieces and crunched underfoot by the rampaging mammoths. Hesitantly, you approach a circle of workers who are looking at the ground.

"Don't look," says Petra as he steps out of the circle and turns you away. "It's Bombax. He had me trapped. Then the mammoths came. We ran, but one of them grabbed Bombax and smashed him to the ground. Clusia and the others saw that and ran away."

"We'll find them all," says Helix, "but we'll let Anomura handle it. Mother's frantic. We need to find her and tell her that everything's all right."

And as you look into his eyes, you know that it is.

THE END

ENDLESS QUEST™ Books

From the producers of the
DUNGEONS & DRAGONS® Game

If you enjoyed this book, look for these additional exciting ENDLESS QUEST™ Books at better bookstores and hobby shops everywhere!

By Rose Estes

#1 **DUNGEON OF DREAD**

#2 **MOUNTAIN OF MIRRORS**

#3 **PILLARS OF PENTEGARN**

#4 **RETURN TO BROOKMERE**

#5 **REVOLT OF THE DWARVES**

#6 **REVENGE OF THE RAINBOW DRAGONS**

#7 **HERO OF WASHINGTON SQUARE**
based on the TOP SECRET®™ Game

By Jean Blashfield

#8 **VILLAINS OF VOLTURNUS**
based on the STAR FRONTIERS™ Game

For a free catalog, write:
TSR Hobbies, Inc.
P.O. Box 756, Dept. EQB
Lake Geneva, WI 53147

TSR Hobbies, Inc.